FOR THE FIRST TIME, DAN'S DETERMINATION TO ESCAPE GAVE WAY TO FEAR.
I'M BEING KIDNAPPED!

THE EMPEROR'S CODE

THE 39 CLUES

GORDON KORMAN

SCHOLASTIC INC.

NEW YORK TORONTO LONDON AUCKLAND
SYDNEY MEXICO CITY NEW DELHI HONG KONG

For Mom, the Cahill behind the curtain
—G.K.

Library of Congress Control Number: 2009937780

ISBN: 978-0-545-06048-6

10 9 8 7 6 5 4 3 2 1   10 11 12 13 14

g e t n o k w i z

Book design and illustration by SJI Associates, Inc.

First edition, April 2010

Printed in China 62

Scholastic US: 557 Broadway • New York, NY 10012
Scholastic Canada: 604 King Street West • Toronto, ON M5V 1E1
Scholastic New Zealand Limited: Private Bag 94407 • Greenmount, Manukau 2141
Scholastic UK Ltd.: Euston House • 24 Eversholt Street • London NW1 1DB

CHAPTER 1

The sneezing began the instant the pet carrier passed the passenger's nose.

A-choo! . . . a-choo! . . . a-choo! . . .

Frozen in the aisle of the British Airways 777, Amy and Dan Cahill waited for the spasm to end. It never did. Instead, the sneezes grew in intensity, each wheezing explosion shaking the poor man's entire body.

"It can't be *that* bad!" Dan said impatiently.

Inside the carrier, Saladin looked around anxiously, unnerved by the ruckus. *"Mrrp?"*

Nellie Gomez, the Cahill kids' au pair, came up behind them. With her iPod blaring the Ramones full blast, all she saw was the man squirming in watery-eyed distress. "I told you the taco stand was serving habanero peppers!" she announced too loudly.

Her booming voice drew the flight attendant to their row. She spoke to the sneezer in Chinese and then turned to Amy and Dan. "It seems Mr. Lee is allergic to cat hair. Your pet will have to ride in the cargo hold."

"But they let us keep him on the connecting flight from Madagascar," Amy protested.

By this time, Nellie had switched off her iPod. "Can't Mr. Lee move to another seat?"

"I'm sorry. The flight is completely full."

Saladin did not go quietly. The Egyptian Mau's outraged *mrrps* resounded through the cabin until the boarding door was closed.

Mr. Lee blew his nose as Amy and Dan squeezed past him into their seats. Nellie settled herself one row behind them, lost once again in her iPod.

"How lame is this?" Dan complained, already fidgeting, even though the plane had yet to pull back from the gate. "Our second million-hour flight in a row, and we don't even have Saladin. What could be worse?"

Their eyes met for about half a second, and then they both looked away. It was a stupid question, and Dan knew it. What could be worse? This was the *definition* of worse—the real reason Dan's mood was misery-minus, and why Amy had no patience for him. It had nothing to do with long flights and cats.

Madrigals!

After all these weeks, Amy and Dan had finally solved the mystery of which branch of the Cahill family they belonged to. Not the scheming and brilliant Lucians, masters of strategy. Not the creative geniuses, the Janus. Not the physically dominant Tomas, descended from warriors. Not the innovative Ekaterinas, the greatest inventors the world has ever known.

No. All these weeks circling the globe in the hunt for the 39 Clues, Amy and Dan had been Madrigals.

Madrigals. The worst of the worst. Madrigals had slaughtered the Russian royal family in the course of a killing spree that spanned continents. Their tools of the trade: stealth, sabotage, deceit, murder, and above all, terror. Even the Lucians feared the Madrigals—and *everyone* was afraid of the Lucians.

It's like living your whole life without ever looking in a mirror, Amy thought, *and suddenly you see your reflection, and you're a monster.*

How could they have been Madrigals without knowing it? All the way from Africa they had repeated that question, hammering themselves with it, hoping against hope that if they asked it enough, the answer might change from the awful truth.

But Madrigals were so secretive that they even kept secrets from themselves. Amy and Dan's grandmother, Grace, must have been a Madrigal, too. After the death of their parents, she'd been their closest relative in the world. Yet she'd never said a word about it to them.

Now Grace is gone, too, Amy reflected sadly. She and Dan were alone—except for Nellie. And, of course, Saladin, their grandmother's cherished pet.

They had barely gotten used to the idea that they were members of the illustrious Cahill family. The search for the 39 Clues still seemed unreal to them—a chance for two Boston orphans to become the most powerful people in human history! Yet this was the ultimate shocker. Their mom and dad must have been Madrigals, too. Did that mean *they* were evil?

Amy had been soul-searching a lot lately, trying to see clearly what was inside her own heart. It wasn't all sweetness and light. Anger at the dirty tricks of the hunt. Isabel—just the name of her parents' killer kindled a heat shimmer that distorted her vision.

Isabel, who had held her as a child. Who had called her *dear* and played the part of the loving aunt.

Isabel, who had taken two happy kids and turned them into orphans . . .

Revenge!! It was more emotional surge than rational thought, the revving of a supercharged engine. It was so automatic, so pure, that it could only have come from the Madrigal at her core.

When you're evil, can you recognize it in yourself?

Aloud, she said to her brother, "Try to sleep. We're going to be jet-lagged like crazy when we get to China."

"I slept all the way from Africa," Dan grumbled.

The plane backed away from the gate, and the safety demonstrations began. *"Shortly after takeoff, we invite you to enjoy the video entertainment on your seat-back screen,"* came the announcement. *"Our first feature film is entitled* Terminator Salvation.*"*

"Yes!" Dan plucked the headphones out of the seat pocket. "Finally, something goes our way!"

"Your dweeb-hood will be studied by future generations," Amy informed him solemnly.

"Don't knock it," he lectured. "Good luck is like a

rash. It spreads. Maybe we'll get on a roll." He popped the phones over his ears as the 777 taxied through the airport traffic, rumbled down the runway, and took off.

London fell away beneath them, yet another city. Mr. Lee clutched his armrest, knuckles whitening with every bump and roll. But Amy and Dan were now experienced flyers who barely noticed the turbulence. In the space of weeks, two kids who had never left New England had visited more than a dozen countries on five different continents.

Dan reclined his chair and focused on the entertainment system in front of him. But when the screen came to life, it showed not the heart-pounding opening of *Terminator Salvation* but scenes of an ornate palace.

"What the—" Dan flipped through the channels. The palace was on every station.

"What's the problem?" Amy hissed.

"Where's the Terminator?"

Amy activated her own screen and peered at the palace scene. "I know this movie—" All at once, her expression softened. "It's *The Last Emperor.* I've seen it two or three times—with Grace."

A lump materialized in her throat. In the heat of the Clue hunt, it was easy to forget that it had been less than two months since Grace Cahill's death.

Grace . . . Madrigal . . . It was no misunderstanding. They'd even seen her secret Madrigal hideout.

I don't care! I loved her . . . still love her . . .

Dan was in no mood for sentimentality. "Man, they

put on the wrong movie!" As he reached for the flight attendant call button, he caught sight of the monitor in front of their allergic neighbor. There was the Terminator, in all his futuristic glory.

In dismay, Dan climbed halfway over the seat back and gawked at the upside-down cyborg on Nellie's screen. "Everybody's getting *Terminator* but us!"

Amy frowned. "Why would only two seats be showing something different?"

"There's an international conspiracy to bore me," mourned her brother.

Beneath the passenger concourses of Heathrow churned a beehive of activity. Down at the tarmac, an army of mechanics and baggage handlers kept one of the world's busiest airports humming.

Several maintenance people were enjoying a tea break when they noticed a new man in the locker room. He was older than the others — probably in his late sixties. As he shrugged out of his coverall, they observed that he was very well dressed in a cashmere blazer, turtleneck, and slacks, all black. Careful scrutiny would have revealed that his ID badge was counterfeit. He did not work here. He did not work anywhere.

Although none of the employees recognized the man in black, Amy and Dan would have. He had dogged their footsteps across more than half the globe.

CHAPTER 2

To Dan, *The Last Emperor* was as boring as the ten-hour flight to Beijing.

"You should pay attention," Amy advised. "This will be good preparation for our trip to China."

"Mmm," he murmured, eyelids heavy. The only good that could come from being cheated out of *Terminator* would be if this lousy film put him to sleep.

He had just dozed off when Amy suddenly dug her fingernails into his arm. "Dan!"

"What's the big idea?" His bleary eyes focused on his sister, who was pointing at the screen. "Come on, Amy. I went to sleep to get *away* from *The Last Emperor*!"

"Look!" Amy insisted. "On that wall!"

Dan squinted. The scene showed the three-year-old Puyi, emperor of China, playing in the Forbidden City, the vast imperial complex. There were hundreds of ornately decorated palaces, temples, and statues. And there, painted on the side of a small building—

"The Janus crest!" he exclaimed in amazement.

Amy frowned. "Why's it in *The Last Emperor*?"

"A lot of showbiz people are Janus," Dan suggested. "Maybe the guy who made this movie was one of them."

"Maybe," his sister said grudgingly, "but I doubt it. *The Last Emperor* was shot in the eighties. The paint on that wall looks a lot older than that."

"But who else could have—?" Dan goggled. "You mean *him*?" He pointed to the toddler clad in royal robes on the screen. "Pee-yoo?"

Amy was disgusted. "The name is Puyi, and he was emperor of China, not a bad smell."

"And you think he comes from one of the Asian branches of the Cahills?"

"It doesn't have to be Puyi," Amy reasoned. "The Forbidden City has existed for centuries. And a lot more people than just emperors have lived there. Don't forget the imperial court, attendants, monks, eunuchs—"

"What's a eunuch?" Dan interrupted.

"Well . . ." Amy blushed, choosing her words carefully. "You know how Saladin was neutered to keep him from making any cat babies—"

"Yeah, but they don't do that to *people*—" Dan's face drained of color. "Do they?"

"In ancient China they did," his sister replied.

Dan was wary. "But they stopped, right?"

She rolled her eyes. "A lot of cultures used to do things we'd consider weird today. Including our own. And anyway, China is where our parents went after they left Africa, and Grace traveled there, too. The movie is even more proof that we're on the right track. Ours are the only two seats on this plane getting *The Last Emperor.* Somebody *wanted* us to see the Janus crest."

"Yeah, but what if it was the competition sending us on a wild goose chase?" Dan asked. "Or the Madrigals, trying to . . ." The skin around his lips tightened to a grimace.

"It's a chance we'll have to take," Amy decided. "At least we know our first stop in Beijing: the Forbidden City, home to China's rulers a half century before Gideon Cahill was even born."

Eyes on the prize. It made sense.

It was also a very Madrigal way of thinking.

The new Beijing terminal was one of the most advanced airport buildings in the world. It was ultramodern, yet distinctly Chinese, the curves of its soaring glass ceiling incorporating ancient colors and designs.

"According to the guidebook, the whole place was inspired by the form of the Chinese dragon," Amy told her travel companions.

Dan's eyes were set on the signs leading to baggage claim. "Let's hope the airline didn't send Saladin to Antarctica."

The pet carrier circled a luggage carousel, partly hidden by much larger suitcases, boxes, and trunks. Outraged mewing could be heard halfway across the international arrivals lobby.

Dan dug the carrier out from beneath a bag of golf clubs. He peered in at the cat. "Chill out, buddy."

He received a sharp *mrrp* of admonishment in return.

As they left the baggage claim, the cat's agitation grew. He clawed nonstop at the mesh of the carrier.

Amy was worried. "What's wrong with Saladin, Dan? Is he sick?"

"He's probably just stir-crazy," Dan replied. "I'm going to cut him loose, let him stretch his legs."

"You can't do that," Nellie protested. "We're in the middle of a crowded airport."

But Dan had already sprung the door.

Saladin burst from the carrier like he'd been shot out of a cannon, claws skittering on the tiles. He spun around, getting his bearings. Then, before their horrified eyes, he launched himself at a tall, lean older man seated on a nearby bench, reading a newspaper.

"Saladin!" Amy gasped. "No!"

A cry of shock escaped the victim, and he leaped to his feet, sending his hat flopping to the floor.

Dan grabbed the cat. Amy picked up the fallen hat and held it out to its owner. "Sorry, mister—" Her eyes fell on his diamond-handled walking stick.

He accepted the hat with a sheepish smile. It was Alistair Oh, Cahill cousin and competitor in the search for the 39 Clues.

"Ah, hello, children. You're looking well."

The Egyptian Mau hissed at him from Dan's arms.

"You were spying on us!" Amy accused.

"Spying?" Uncle Alistair repeated. "No. I'm merely here to welcome you back to Asia and offer my assistance.

The language barrier can be quite a hurdle in China, but my Mandarin is excellent."

Nellie's eyes narrowed the way they always did when she suspected her charges were being taken advantage of. "And you're making this offer out of the goodness of your heart?"

"Of course! Although"—Alistair's gracious smile began to seem slightly forced—"it would be an excellent opportunity to bring one another up to date on our progress on the clue hunt."

"Aha!" Dan exploded. "You only want to help so you can steal our clues because you know you're *losing*!"

The smile disappeared, and Amy and Dan noticed their distant cousin's exhausted, red-rimmed eyes.

"I'm afraid, children, that we all might be losing," he admitted. "Ian and Natalie Kabra have been in China for several days already. Even more worrisome, the Holts have completely dropped off the radar screen."

"Try the Mr. Universe contest," Dan suggested.

Alistair regarded him ruefully. "We've all underestimated the Holts. In Ekat circles, the rumor is that they've made a major breakthrough. It's not too late to catch them—*if* we work together."

Amy's eyes locked with her brother's. Of all their competitors in the contest, Uncle Alistair was the only one who felt like family. True, he had betrayed them—and more than just once. But out of their Cahill cousins, Alistair alone seemed to care what happened to them.

The image of Uncle Alistair faded in Amy's mind,

to be replaced by a much darker picture. That terrible night years before; the fire that had killed their parents. Alistair had been there.

Amy's eyes filled with tears. *Stop thinking about it!*

Alistair was no murderer. At worst, he had been Isabel's unwitting accomplice. Still, it would take a lot for her to confide in him. And as for Dan . . .

"Why can't you just lie and cheat like the others?" Dan snapped. "Can't you see that's better than being nice one minute and then turning around and selling us out? It may be very Cahill, but it *stinks*! Grace had a saying: Fool me once, shame on you; fool me twice, I'll conk you with this pet carrier!"

"You must reconsider," Alistair began urgently.

Nellie spoke up. "The kids said it's not happening."

"Yes, but—"

Dan let go of Saladin, and the Egyptian Mau pounced on Alistair's ankles. There was a ripping sound as the cat's claws removed most of the left cuff from Alistair's custom-tailored dress slacks. Fabric flapping, the old fellow hightailed it to the exit.

"If you change your mind, I'm at the Imperial Hotel," he tossed over his shoulder, and was gone.

Nellie put an arm around her two charges. "I hope you knuckleheads have a plan, now that you've sent Alistair packing."

Amy manufactured a nervous smile. "Next stop—the Gate of Heavenly Peace."

CHAPTER 3

The 39 Clues may have been a high-stakes treasure hunt with world domination as the prize. But sooner or later you always ended up in some dumb museum.

Sad but true, Dan thought as the smiling tour guide led them through vast halls filled with floor-to-ceiling display cases. The Palace Museum inside the Forbidden City held more than three hundred thousand ceramic and porcelain pieces alone.

"You could have soup in a different bowl every day for, like, a thousand years," he whispered to Amy.

"This is the greatest art collection I've ever seen," she marveled, missing his wisecrack. "Even better than the Janus stronghold in Venice!"

"Those emperors were Cahills, all right," Dan decided. "Totally loaded—like everybody else in the family except us."

Amy's brow knit. "The emperors lived here for six centuries. How do we know which generation was involved in the clue hunt?"

"Our parents must have had an idea," Dan put in.

"Why else would they come here after Africa?"

She nodded. "Good point. Let's listen to the tour guide. We might learn something important."

Dan groaned. Like there was going to be a Clue in the butterfly pattern on an old chamber pot. They already knew what they were looking for — the crest from *The Last Emperor*. It was out there somewhere, faded but still visible, on the wall of one of these buildings.

Dan checked his watch. Still more than three hours to go before they were meeting Nellie, who was off with Saladin, looking for a hotel. And no chance of pushing the time up. None of their new phones had service in China. They were trapped here with three hundred thousand plates.

"This collection began in the Ming dynasty, but the size increased greatly during the Qing," the guide was saying. "The Qing emperors were renowned for their obsessive commitment to the arts. . . ."

"That's it!" Amy hissed.

"That's what?"

"Obsessed with art? Does that sound familiar?"

Dan was beginning to clue in. "The Janus! Those guys would trade their mothers for a painting!"

Amy's eyes were alight with excitement. "Dan, it's all coming together. Whatever brought our parents to China — it has something to do with the Janus branch. Something *big*."

Dan nodded. "But how are we going to find the Janus crest if we're stuck doing the dishes?"

Amy took in the walkie-talkie dangling from the guide's belt. "If that guy sees us sneaking away, he'll call security. Besides, we don't know where to look. The Forbidden City is the largest palace complex in the world. There are more than nine hundred buildings!"

Dan opened their brochure to the grounds plan of the 180-acre Forbidden City. "I think I remember the movie. If I can figure out which way to tilt this map—" He shifted the page, studying it intently. Dan had a photographic memory, but coordinating film scenes with a printed diagram was tricky. "Let's see, the doo-hickey of supreme whatchamacallit is over *there*—"

"Hall of Supreme Harmony," Amy corrected.

"—so I bet the Janus crest should be somewhere in *this* section, over by the whatchamacallit of tranquil thingamajig."

"Palace of Tranquil Longevity," Amy supplied.

"I'll find it," Dan decided. "Okay, you create a diversion—"

His sister was nervous. "What diversion? I can't do cartwheels in here. Something could get broken."

"Yeah," Dan said, "you wouldn't want these guys to run out of plates. It's not rocket science. Just go to the other side of the group and start asking boring questions. And while he's giving you boring answers, I'll slip away."

"Fine," she replied, sounding only a little miffed at his word choice. She raised her hand. "Ex-ex—" *Stop it,* she commanded herself. Her stammer often came out at moments of stress, but this was *important*. "Excuse me, how old are those pieces — no, *these* over here —"

Amy had chosen well. A line of tall glass cases separated Dan from the group. It was no problem for him to slip out of the room. His sister was annoying, but he had to admit they made a pretty good team.

Not bad for a couple of Madrigals, he reflected, and immediately regretted the thought.

It was no joke. In Africa they'd learned that the aliases on their parents' passports — Mr. and Mrs. Nudelman — matched the names of a notorious pair of murderers and thieves. Mom and Dad — the Bonnie and Clyde of the Southern Hemisphere? Ridiculous. A coincidence. And yet . . .

Husband and wife . . . ruthless killers . . . Madrigals . . .

Just the thought of it made his shoulders sag.

He got lost a few times sneaking out of the building, wandering through the labyrinth of ornate rooms. At last, he managed to find an entrance and stepped out into the Forbidden City. It was an immense complex, with five ginormous palaces and seventeen that counted as merely huge — not to mention nearly a thousand smaller buildings of various shapes and sizes. The temples, monuments, and gardens seemed to go on forever. It really was a *city* — as if half of downtown Boston had all been built for one guy to live in. But this was far more colorful than any part of Boston — a kaleidoscope of imperial yellow, rich red, and glittering gold leaf.

Everything screamed wealth and luxury beyond imagination. Yet despite the size of the place, Dan couldn't escape a shut-in feeling — the four massive outer gates, the high walls, the observation towers at the corners. He tried to picture Puyi — the kid emperor from the movie — having all this as his personal playground. According to the tour guide, Puyi had officially abdicated at age six, but the Chinese government let him stay here until he was a young man.

Using the Gate of Heavenly Peace as a point of reference, Dan got his bearings and headed for the area he remembered from *The Last Emperor*. He knew a moment of uncertainty. Was he searching in China for a crest that was really six thousand miles away on a Hollywood soundstage?

Too late to worry about that now . . .

Soon he was in a section of smaller, lower buildings. Even though the Forbidden City had been the emperor's home, there had been plenty of attendants, monks, and — ouch — eunuchs who'd lived there, too. Maybe this was their neighborhood. As he began to pass between the rows, scanning walls for the Janus crest, he wondered how high up on the trouble scale it would be to get caught here. There were no tourists around, and also no security. Everybody seemed to be at Plates "R" Us, either looking at dishes or guarding them.

Dan forged on. Artwork, designs, and calligraphy surrounded him on pillars, signs, and walls. A very Janus place, for sure. So where was the crest?

A feeling of deep dread took hold in the pit of his stomach. This was their only lead. If they couldn't find it, they'd be left wandering around a vast country of more than a billion people without the faintest idea what they were looking for.

Frustration melted into alarm. He'd miscalculated somehow. Maybe his photographic memory wasn't as photographic as he'd thought. He spun around desperately. Nothing! Except—

Around the corner, on the wall of a small temple, his eyes fell on a shape that didn't belong. The letter S.

Everything else is in Chinese. What's an S doing there?

The paint was old and washed out, barely visible anymore. He squinted at the wall . . . and suddenly he was looking right at it.

It wasn't an S at all! It was the curled tail of an animal—a picture that had faded over the years, bleached by sun and worn by weather. A standing wolf in a fighting pose, glancing over its shoulder.

Symbol of the Janus branch!

CHAPTER 4

Dan could barely restrain himself from letting out a whoop that would have shattered every dish in the museum.

Calm down. Finding the crest is the easy part.

The trick was to figure out what it meant.

The original temple had an open entrance, but in modern times a metal gate had been installed to keep intruders out. Cautiously, he edged up to the chain mesh and peered inside. The interior reminded him of a house right after movers had driven off with the entire contents — a hollow shell. It was empty, except for dust and a few crickets.

He examined the barrier critically. He could probably break in somehow, but why bother? There didn't seem to be anything here. Besides, his sister would go nuts if he defiled a four-hundred-year-old temple. He smiled in spite of himself. For her, it was a short trip.

He stepped back off the wooden porch, watching the crickets on the sloped roof.

This place could use a Roach Motel, he reflected.

Was there such a thing as a Cricket Motel?

And then one of the insects *disappeared*.

Huh? He paid closer attention. There must have been an opening in the roof tiles that the crickets were crawling in and out of.

He returned to the security gate and peered inside. The temple ceiling was low, almost claustrophobic. Yet the roof was a tall A-frame. . . .

An attic! A secret attic!

With a furtive look around to confirm he was alone, he climbed onto the porch rail and began to shinny up the corner post to the eaves. A moment's hesitation — unobserved also meant there'd be no one to call an ambulance if he fell off the building. Mustering his strength, he reached past the overhang and hoisted himself onto the steep roof, holding on like Spider-Man to the ancient yellow tile shingles.

He clung there for a moment, catching his breath and listening to the steady pounding of his heart. No, wait — that wasn't his heartbeat! It was the *thrum, thrum, thrum* of marching feet. He flattened himself on the steep sloping roof and tried to disappear.

In the pathway below, a unit of six soldiers trooped by in close-order formation. Security? No, they were dressed in red silk tunics with matching hats — like palace guards from back in the day when the emperors lived here. This was a ceremonial parade. The soldiers were trained to keep their eyes riveted straight ahead and never noticed the intruder on the roof.

As they disappeared into the maze of crimson walls, Dan allowed his body to relax. And that was something you should never do on a steep incline.

He was sliding before he even noticed. Frantically, he scrabbled for a handhold, to no avail. He was skidding slowly but inexorably toward a long drop.

In desperation, he tried to wedge his fingers into the gap in a broken tile — anything to gain some leverage. With the creak of rusty hinges, a section of shingles came away from the roof, opening like a mailbox.

He hung there, stopped at last, his astonishment turning to triumph. A trapdoor! This was the way in.

The discovery brought a hidden reserve of strength. Dan hauled himself up and over the lip of the opening and dropped down onto a dusty wooden floor.

The chirping was all around him like church bells, so loud that he felt it below the line of his gums. Crickets. Thousands of them. The floor and walls crawled.

Instinctively, he reached for the inhaler in his pocket. *No,* he told himself. *You don't get an asthma attack from being grossed out.*

With effort, he forced away his revulsion and examined the hidden compartment.

The attic was narrow, with decent headroom only at the center. In the corners, he had to duck. The place was empty except for the crickets. Could crickets be the Clue? That made zero sense. There was no way these crickets could date back to some Chinese emperor.

Then he realized that the place wasn't empty after

all. On the floor in the far corner lay a piece of fabric about the size of a hand towel. He stooped and picked it up, shaking off several crickets and a puff of dust. It was a dull gold sheet of silk covered in Chinese calligraphy, with a large red signature stamp — a "chop," the tour guide had called it.

He looked closer in the dim light. It wasn't all Chinese characters. With mounting excitement, he recognized the symbols for the four branches of his illustrious family, as well as the Cahill crest.

His brow furrowed. The symbols were laid out like a mathematical equation:

There was no question about it. This object was what had brought them to the Forbidden City. He had to get it back to Amy so they could figure out what it meant.

"Later, dudes," he breathed to the chirping crickets. He folded the piece of silk and stuffed it into his shirt. Then he stretched for the opening above and hauled himself back onto the roof.

He was extra careful on the way down, pressing himself into the tiles as he shut the trapdoor. He practically oozed to the pillar that was his safe passage back to ground level. Perhaps he should have used some of that great care to scout the area first. For when he set foot on the pathway, he found himself in the grip of a uniformed guard. And this one wasn't wearing the ceremonial garb of centuries past. His jacket bore the red star insignia of the Chinese army.

The man barked something in his own language, then took in Dan's Western features and switched to English. "This area is restricted!"

"I lost my tour group—" Dan began.

The officer began to pat him down, pausing at the soft bulge under his shirt.

"What is this?" He pulled out the folded silk.

Dan's mind worked at light speed. *If he sees the writing inside, he'll never let me keep it.*

With a wheeze, he sucked back all the dust of the attic that had found its way into his nasal passages. Then he snatched the silk out of the officer's hand and unloaded a mighty sneeze into it.

The man grimaced. "Where are your parents?"

"Dead," Dan replied, sticking the silk back under his shirt. "I'm here with my sister, and I got lost."

"You lie. I saw you climbing down from the roof of this structure."

"I wanted a better view. I was trying to find the museum so I could go back."

The man scoffed and indicated the immense roof of the main palace towering over the Forbidden City. "The museum is difficult to miss."

"I've got a lousy sense of direction," Dan said.

"You are rude, young man. You are also—how do they say it in your language? Ah, yes—busted."

CHAPTER 5

Amy walked with the rest of her tour group toward the Gate of Heavenly Peace, wondering if Dan had located the mysterious Janus crest they had spotted in the movie.

The tiny twists of fortune that spelled the difference between discovering a Clue and being left clueless could be so minor. It would almost be funny—if the fate of the world didn't hang in the balance.

As for the thought of her eleven-year-old brother on the loose in the Forbidden City—well, it made her nervous, but she was learning to live with it. Over the past weeks, the two of them had survived near misses that made this seem like playtime at day care. Anyway, they would be reunited when they met Nellie in—she consulted her watch—half an hour. She hoped the au pair had found them a decent hotel.

The thought made her frown. Lately, there had been hints that Nellie might be more than she seemed.

Or maybe I'm just getting paranoid. . . .

She had no trouble believing that paranoia was very

THE 39 CLUES

24

Madrigal. Her parents had been paranoid—and with good reason. Everybody *had* been out to get them.

And one had succeeded.

Yet even with their small children, Mom and Dad had been strangely secretive. Thinking back, there had always been rules—keep out of the basement or a certain closet; don't open that crate or that duffel bag. Only now did it occur to her to wonder what they'd been hiding—black-market grenades, a severed head, uranium 235, the Ebola virus, the lost remains of Wolfgang Amadeus Mozart. They were "Nudelmans," after all. She cringed as if shrinking from something horrible. She had so few memories of her parents, and now even the tiny scraps that were left had to be put through the Madrigal detector—every word, every gesture scanned for signs of evil. How pathetic was that?

A member of her tour interrupted her tortured reverie. "Excuse me, dear, but isn't that your little brother over there? Why does that soldier have him in handcuffs?"

Just inside the gate stood an angry-looking man in a military uniform, with Dan in custody.

Amy rushed forward. "What are you doing to my brother?"

The guard spoke up. "You are in charge of this boy? You yourself are a child."

"We're meeting our au pair in Tiananmen Square," Amy explained. "Dan, what happened?"

Dan winked at her and shrugged. "I couldn't find

you, so I climbed up on some temple for a better view. And this guy got all bent out of shape about it."

The guard reddened and unlocked the cuffs. "You will leave and never return."

"How about that," Dan said mildly as they were escorted through the Gate of Heavenly Peace, across the footbridge, and over the moat. "Forbidden from the Forbidden City. Oh, well, if you have to get forbidden, I suppose this is the place for it."

"Very funny," Amy hissed as they crossed the boulevard into Tiananmen Square. She shuddered. Considering the vast size of the square, it was packed with people. Amy didn't like crowds—and here she was in the most crowded place in the most crowded country on earth. "Now we can't go back and look for—"

"I've already got it," Dan said, removing the folded silk from inside his shirt. "Here, hold it by the edges. I had to blow my nose in it so Mr. Happy would think it was a handkerchief." He handed it to her.

Amy nearly dropped it. "You put *snot* on the clue?"

Dan was annoyed. "You want to see it or not?"

Amy unwrapped the soiled, wrinkled silk, keeping it hidden from curious passersby in the bustling square. In the bright sun, they could see that the pale gold silk was overlaid with a pattern of butterflies:

将你追求的,握在手中,
于出生一刻已註定,
在天地相交處。

溥仪

"'Lucian plus Janus plus Tomas plus Ekat equals Cahill,'" she recited aloud. "What could that mean? That if you add up the branches you've got the whole family?"

"If that's the big message," Dan concluded, "then it wasn't worth getting arrested. That's like saying hearts, spades, diamonds, and clubs make a deck of cards."

"What's this shape?" Amy traced a line that circled the Lucian crest. "There's one around each symbol, including the Cahill coat of arms."

Dan frowned. "I wish we could translate some of this writing."

"Uncle Alistair knows Chinese," Amy mused.

"No way!" Dan was adamant. "I'm never trusting that guy again! We *know* he was with Mom and Dad the night Isabel set the fire!"

Amy tried to choose her words carefully. "You know, Dan, I've been thinking about something that won't go away."

Dan was alarmed. "I don't like that look on your face. It usually means I have to do research on Mozart or Howard Carter or some other boring dead guy."

"Be serious," she chided gently. "There's something pretty big we have to face up to." She took a deep breath. "Mom and Dad were Madrigals. Did it ever occur to you that the fire had something to do with that?"

Dan was wide-eyed. "You don't think they helped Isabel burn their own house down!"

"Of course not. But who knows what kind of weird stuff a couple of Madrigals could have been into? We look at the other teams as the bad guys. But what if, back then, that's how the rest of the family saw Mom and Dad? A couple of loose cannons who had to be stopped?"

Dan was horrified. "You're saying they died because they had it coming?"

"Not exactly that, but—"

"You *are*! That's *exactly* what you're saying!" Dan reddened. "This clue hunt has turned your brains to cole slaw! That's our parents you're talking about! How can you even consider it?"

"You think it's easy for me?" Amy shot back. "You

were four when they died. You barely remember them."

"You don't own their memory!" Dan shot back. "Not even a four-year-old forgets when the fire chief tells him his parents are never coming back. If I close my eyes, I can still see the guy! He has a mustache and a big ring on his finger, and he's showing Grace what's left of that copper sculpture, the one with the bug on it!"

"Bug?"

"That's exactly what he said!" Dan insisted. "You know how things stick in my mind! I'd bet my life on it!"

"And you remember seeing a *bug*?" Amy probed.

"No. Only hearing the words. The bug must have burned up in the fire."

"Then how would the fire chief know about it?"

Dan stared at her. "Ask *him*!"

"Don't you see?" Amy demanded. "He wasn't talking about an *insect*. It must have been a listening device! Our house was bugged—by Isabel, probably."

"So what?" Dan argued. "She burned the place to the ground with two people inside! She's sick! Planting a bug would be kid stuff!"

"The point is that our memories of our parents are so distant we can't rely on them," Amy said in a choked voice. "If a bug can turn out to be a listening device, there's no telling how much we got confused. Did we *really* know Mom and Dad? They were up to their necks in the thirty-nine clues; we had no idea. They were Madrigals, and even today, we don't understand how bad that could be. Face it, Dan. We *never* knew them."

Dan was so angry that his face radiated heat. "Speak for yourself! I know them just fine! I know they were great people! I know they didn't deserve to die young! And I know they *definitely* didn't deserve to have a daughter like you trashing their memory!"

"In Africa it's the memory of two serial killers! Down there, people would be *relieved* to know they're dead, and — and —" Her voice cracked.

He stuck out his chin, daring her to say it. "And what?"

"And maybe we should be, too," Amy blurted.

In that instant, Dan Cahill knew what it was to be a booster rocket — white-hot combustion converting to pure motion, thrusting you forward. He launched himself at her, fists balled, ready to fight. But at the point of attack, he found he couldn't hit her, couldn't even yell at her. All he could do was run away.

"Come back!" she cried anxiously.

At last he found words, the only three he could bring himself to utter to the sister he no longer knew. *"I hate you!"*

He bumped into a tourist focusing a camera, side-stepped, kept on going. Anything to put distance between himself and Amy.

Her voice was distant now. "Don't get lost! Nellie will be here in twenty minutes!"

Lost! he seethed. Amy was the one who was lost. If you spent enough time hanging around Cahills, eventually you ended up just like them. What a sorry bunch, squabbling over who was going to rule the world by out-backstabbing the backstabbers! And now Amy was right up there with the worst of them.

How could she say stuff like that? They had so little of their parents — barely more than a few fading recollections — a kiss, a touch, a burst of laughter. Amy was tarnishing all that. And for what? The Clue hunt!

I've got to get off this treadmill before it makes a traitor of me, too! I quit!

The sheer gravity of the decision brought him up short. He and his sister had nearly gotten killed for this contest. They had given up two million dollars to be a part of it. It was a chance to shape human history — to become the most powerful Cahills of all time!

Cahill, shmahill! I've already had enough of the Cahills to last a thousand centuries. I wish my name was Finkelstein! I'm out!

Could you do that? Could a guy just secede from the Cahill family? Leaving the Clue hunt would be easy. All he had to do was stop searching. But he'd always be a Cahill. The family knew it. Isabel Kabra knew it — he'd never be free of the danger from his crazy relatives.

He stumbled across the square, slaloming around classes of children on field trips, business people on break, senior citizens doing calisthenics and tai chi, tourists, and small patrols of police and military. The chatter of conversation was everywhere, much of it on cell phones, which everyone seemed to have. For the first time since arriving in China, he really had a sense of being at the center of the busiest, most populated nation on earth.

A plan — that was it. He needed a post–39 Clues plan. He'd gone straight from his regular life to Grace's funeral to the contest. What was next? Aunt Beatrice? Not an option. The US Embassy? No good, that just led to Aunt Beatrice. Amy?

I'll never forgive her for what she said!

He turned back to glare at her, but his view of Amy was obstructed by a wedding party crossing the square. Instead of a rented limo, the bride and groom rode in old-fashioned sedan chairs, sliding doors drawn.

What's a Boston kid doing in this bizarre, alien place, ten thousand miles from Fenway?

Disoriented as he was, he had to admit this was the best way to travel in Beijing — carried around by bearers who toted you, unjostled, through the crowds in Tiananmen Square. The first chair brushed by close enough for Dan to see the grain in the painted wood. The second stopped directly in front of him. He stared in amazement as the sliding panel was swept aside.

It happened so fast that it was all over by the time Dan had the chance to register any alarm. Two strong arms reached out and hauled him inside. Then his captor jumped down to the square, slammed the door shut, and joined the bearers who were carrying the chair. Before Dan could protest, he was hoisted up and moving quickly.

"Hey!" Desperately, Dan worked at the slider, but it

was locked in place. He pounded on the wooden panel. "Let me out!"

No one paid any attention. In fact, he seemed to be gathering speed, jolted along as the bearers broke into a run. A horn honked; traffic noise. They were out of the square, moving along the city streets.

Dan pressed his back against the side of the compartment and kicked frantically at the closed slider. The chair shook, but the panel held firm. He got up to a crouch and slammed his shoulder against the wall. Pain stabbed through his upper body. He fought through it, pounding ever harder. There were shouts of agitation from the bearers, but their distress never even slowed them down.

For the first time, Dan's determination to escape gave way to fear.

I'm being kidnapped!

CHAPTER 6

A minute ago, he'd been so furious with Amy that their argument had filled his every thought. Now, in the blink of an eye, the entire world had changed.

He resumed his struggle, banging and shouting. He couldn't blast his way out, but the fuss he was kicking up might attract someone's attention—maybe even a cop's.

After ten minutes of it, he was sweat-soaked and exhausted—so much so that he almost didn't notice when the sedan chair stopped and was lowered to ground level. A new plan formed in Dan's mind. The instant that door opened, somebody was going to get a memorable kick in the head. And while the guy was picking up his teeth, Dan would be out of there and gone.

There was a clicking sound as the panel was unlocked. He tensed, ready for action. His foot was already coming forward as the slider eased open.

There was no one to kick. Instead, he was looking at the interior of a van. Suddenly, the sedan chair tilted, and he was dumped into the cargo bay. The van's door shut, and the vehicle screeched away, burning rubber.

Enraged, Dan managed to get to his knees for the first glimpse of his captors.

"Is that you, or is the air pollution in Beijing as bad as they say?" sniffed Natalie Kabra.

Dan drew in a shocked breath. Natalie's olive skin was darker than her mother's, but the two shared the same chiseled features — classic beauty camouflaging merciless, piercing eyes. In the case of Isabel, the eyes of a murderer.

Natalie and her older brother, Ian, peered disdainfully back at him over the cargo partition. Dan looked around anxiously — no Isabel, at least, not in the van. The only other occupant was on a jump seat in the rear with Dan — a huge man, obviously the Kabras' hired goon.

Dan wasn't going to give his Lucian cousins the satisfaction of knowing he was scared. "No limo today?" he sneered. "What, you maxed out your credit cards in Africa?"

Ian turned to the driver. "Stop short."

The man slammed on the brakes, and the van bucked to a halt, sending Dan flying into the cargo partition. He came up stunned, lip swelling.

"So Alistair was right," Dan groaned. "You guys *are* in China."

"We're everywhere," Natalie purred. "And rest assured we're always several steps ahead of you two charity cases and your freakish babysitter."

"Au pair," Dan corrected automatically.

"Yes, we're in China," Ian said impatiently. "And so are you. Now explain to me what you were doing inside that temple in the Forbidden City."

"Don't know what you're talking about," Dan mumbled stubbornly.

Ian nodded agreeably. "I thought that might be your answer. This is the part where Mr. Chen helps you remember."

With the smile of a man who enjoys his work, the goon reached out, grabbed Dan by the collar, and hoisted him in the air.

"Okay, okay!" Dan gave in. What was the point of taking a beating? Amy had the silk, so it was safe from these vultures. Besides, Dan was out of the contest. He didn't care if he never saw another Clue in his life. "Yeah, I broke into the temple because there was a Janus crest on the outside wall."

"And what did you find?" Natalie probed, voice silky, expression ruthless.

"Crickets," Dan replied. "About forty billion of them. Ugly suckers — like you two."

"Anything else?" Ian demanded with a gesture at Mr. Chen.

The goon twisted Dan's arm in a hammerlock and applied subtle pressure. The pain was unlike anything Dan had ever experienced before. It was a shattering agony that erased all thoughts but one: *Make this stop.*

Still, he held back. *If they know about the silk, that'll sic them on Amy. . . .*

Angry as he was with his sister, he couldn't do that to her.

"Tell us the truth!" Ian ordered, his composure slightly broken.

"Calm down," Natalie soothed. "No one can resist Mr. Chen's built-in lie detector test."

"What do you know about the Holts?" Ian persisted.

Dan saw no harm in replying. "Uncle Alistair's all freaked out about them. He says they've found a lead none of the rest of us have."

"What lead?" Ian fairly exploded.

His sister was patient. "If he knew, then obviously it wouldn't be a lead that nobody else has."

"Hilarious," Ian muttered. "It won't be so funny if we lose to those gorillas! Can you imagine a world with them in charge?"

Natalie sighed her agreement. "I guess we'll have to search the urchin just in case. And me without my flea powder . . ."

But besides an inhaler, a few bills from three different continents, and a dead cricket, there was nothing to be found.

Mr. Chen placed a chloroform-soaked handkerchief over Dan's nose and mouth. Dan held his breath and put up a struggle, but a sharp chemical smell, somewhere between hospital antiseptic and rubbing alcohol, penetrated his defenses. His vision began to darken around the edges as the interior of the van receded from him.

"Can't . . ." He tried to claw back, but it was no use. He was falling.

"Nighty-night," Natalie whispered.

Dan's last thought before blackness claimed him: *I never realized how much she sounds like her mother.*

Saladin was munching contentedly on a shrimp dumpling when Nellie carried him through Tiananmen Square to the appointed meeting place in front of the Gate of Heavenly Peace.

She spotted Amy and marched right up to her. "I got us a pretty good hotel right off the main drag—which I can't pronounce. It isn't luxe, but the chef in the restaurant is kind of cute. And he makes a bird's nest soup to die for." She looked around. "Where's Dan?"

Amy's expression was tragic. "Gone."

"What do you mean 'gone'? Gone where?"

Amy shrugged miserably. "We had a big fight and he took off."

Nellie sighed tolerantly. "Save me from these Cahills! Bad enough your whole family is in a perpetual state of warfare; you have to start something up with your brother."

"Sorry," Amy mumbled. She had to hold herself back from spilling the beans about the argument she'd had with Dan. Not that it would change anything, but the idea that someone else knew might help her feel a little less alone.

And yet—how would she even begin to describe it? The feelings about Mom and Dad were just too personal and too painful. Aside from a few dusty memories, all they had of their parents was the belief that Hope and Arthur had been *good*. To lose that—

No wonder Dan couldn't handle it.

Her words came back to haunt her. She had suggested they should be glad their parents were dead.

Harsh. True or not, it was a cruel thing to say. *Madrigal* cruel.

This is my fault. I drove him away.

She swallowed hard. "He wouldn't go far, right?"

"Let's search the square," Nellie decided.

They did—for two solid hours. Dan was nowhere to be found.

"I'll kill him!" Amy threatened. "He's doing this on purpose just to make me nuts!"

Nellie's face was whitening steadily as she scanned the crowd. "Where can he be?"

"Mrrp," put in Saladin pointedly.

The au pair regarded the cat with annoyance. "How can you think of food at a time like this? Dan's missing."

"Never underestimate Dan's capacity to disappear just to be a rotten kid," Amy put in.

Nellie was more serious. "I don't think so. He has

no Chinese money, no clothes to change into, no place to sleep—he doesn't even have his laptop, and you know how much he loves that. I have to admit I'm worried."

"Animals have a good sense of smell," Amy suggested. "Maybe Saladin can be like a bloodhound." She took the belt from her jeans and looped it through the cat's collar, forming a makeshift leash. Then she took out the silk that had been inside Dan's shirt and held it to the cat's nose. "Come on, Saladin. Find Dan."

Nellie sat Saladin on the pavement, and the Egyptian Mau took off across the square. He was moving so fast that the girls had to run to keep up with him.

"Good boy!" Amy urged. "He's on the scent!"

They drew a lot of curious glances—two Westerners scrambling behind a cat on a leash. The threesome left Tiananmen Square and headed east on Dong Chang'an Jie. That was where Saladin's destination became clear. He led them straight to a sidewalk food vendor selling dumplings. There, he took his place in line behind the current customer, waiting his turn.

Nellie clucked disapprovingly. "For a cat, you're a pretty big pig."

"Mrrp!"

At last, Amy was able to step back from her short-term irritation and see the big picture.

Something's happened to Dan.

CHAPTER 7

The headache came first, and it was awful—a pounding behind his right eye that would not quit. The whole room seemed to thrum in rhythm with his pain—or, wait! Maybe it was his pain thrumming with the room. What was that noise?

And why was his bed *moving*?

He sat up with a start and very nearly toppled off the conveyor belt to the factory floor forty feet below.

What the—

It all came back to him—being kidnapped, interrogated, and chloroformed by the Kabras. They must have dumped him here—in one of the factories that made China the industrial engine of the entire world!

He took stock of the situation. Behind him and in front of him on the belt were large sheets of multicolored plastic. About ten yards ahead, the pieces were being dropped into a hopper that fed a gigantic stamping machine beneath it. The closer he got, the louder the noise, until it threatened to jar loose his molars.

All remaining grogginess disappeared in a heartbeat.

I'm going to get stamped into the door-crasher special at Walmart!

The only way off the conveyor belt was a four-story drop. And there was no point in yelling for help. No one could possibly hear him over the general din. He had to find a way to stop this belt!

He jumped up and ran against the direction of the conveyor. Every time he came to a sheet of plastic, he crammed it under the belt, hoping to disrupt its operation. There was no result at first, but he refused to despair. This giant machine was never going to run out of plastic. And he was never going to run out of energy to use it to jam the conveyor.

Not unless I want a one-way trip through the guts of that machine!

When he felt the first wobble, he was so encouraged that he found the strength to speed up his efforts. The burning rubber smell came next, and soon he had to watch his footing on the pitching belt. Smoke began to surround him, and the automatic sprinkler system came on. A moment later, the conveyor ground to a halt, and the stamping machine fell silent.

A hooray died in Dan's throat as dozens of factory workers began scaling a system of catwalks toward his position.

Now that the belt had stopped, he could see that the only other way down was on the stamping machine itself. A system of grips and ladders for maintenance workers traced a route up its steel flank. He ran to the end of the belt and swung himself down to a metal ring. From there, it was like the rock wall at the community center back in Massachusetts — a simple matter of finding the right handholds and footholds.

As he jumped to the floor, he nearly tripped over a pallet piled high with the factory's finished product — a mechanical lollipop holder with a figure as its base. All this equipment, all these workers, this giant manufacturing complex, for lollipops. Sheesh.

He picked one up and almost swallowed his tongue. The figure was none other than his Cahill cousin Jonah Wizard, reality TV star, hip-hop mogul, and rival in the Clue hunt. Jonah's smirking face routinely appeared on posters, magazines, action figures, Pez dispensers, lunch boxes, and now motorized lollipop holders. There was no escaping the guy.

He pressed a small button on the base. The candy twirled, and Jonah's tinny voice announced, *"What's happening, yo?"*

Those recorded words turned out to be Dan's undoing. A very agitated foreman grabbed him by the arm. In a few seconds, he was surrounded by a small army of irate factory workers, all yelling at him in Chinese.

He took a lick of the lollipop and tried to look like a passing tourist. *"Mmm — grape. My favorite."*

The foreman switched to heavily accented English. "What you do, boy? You break everything!"

"Check out the conveyor up top," Dan advised. "The belt got a little jammed. Happens a lot, right?"

"*Never* happens!" thundered the foreman. "You spoil perfect record on day of very important visitor!"

"What's happening, yo?" came Jonah Wizard's voice again.

Dan stared at the lollipop holder in his hand. He hadn't pressed the button. . . .

The angry crowd melted away and went to surround the newcomer.

Dan goggled. It was the real Jonah Wizard, live and in person, touring the factory where his lollipops were made. No wonder the Kabras had dumped Dan here. It was a message not just to Dan, but to Jonah, too. He recalled Natalie's words: *We're everywhere. . . .*

The hip-hop star's eyes widened when he spotted Dan. A half step behind him, his ever-present father began composing an e-mail on his BlackBerry.

"Mr. Wizard!" the foreman exclaimed. "Thousand apologies! Worthless boy break machine—"

"Chill, man." Jonah somehow managed to imbue his street lingo with an easygoing, almost folksy simplicity. The world's first down-home hip-hop star. "The kid's my cousin. I told him to meet me here. My fault."

Dan's eyes narrowed even as he sighed with relief. The last time he and Amy had seen Jonah, the creep had marooned them on a crocodile-infested island in the middle of the Nile.

"Where's your sis and the nanny?" Jonah asked.

"Au pair," Dan corrected. "We got—separated."

Jonah shrugged. "It's all good. Chinese TV gave us a

limo to use while we're in town. I'll have the driver give you a ride back to your hotel." He noted the anxious flush on Dan's cheeks. "I get it. You're lost, and you don't know where to find them."

"I can take care of myself," Dan said.

"Word," Jonah agreed. "But why should you have to? We're family. I got you."

"Like you had my back in Egypt?" Dan retorted.

The star looked sheepish. "I feel bad about that. It wasn't cool, but, seriously, I wasn't trying to kill you. I was just slowing you down a little."

"More like trying to turn us into Purina Crocodile Chow."

"Not true, yo. I knew you and your sis could handle yourselves around a few crocs." Jonah took in the wary expression on Dan's face, then turned to his father. "Pops, have our people call every hotel and see if They can track down Amy Cahill and—and—"

"Nellie Gomez," Dan supplied.

"Don't stress, cuz," Jonah soothed. "We'll find them. In the meantime, you can kick it with us."

Dan thought it over. He doubted Amy and Nellie would still be in Tiananmen Square, and he had no idea where they were staying. *Right now, Mr. Wizard has a better chance of finding them than I do. . . .*

By then, the sprinklers had been shut off, and the workers were repairing the conveyor belt. Dan allowed himself to be taken on the factory tour with Jonah, the two of them licking at motorized lollipops.

After the factory, they boarded Jonah's stretch Hummer and traveled to the mammoth Lufthansa Friendship Shopping Center.

When the staff saw the international reality TV star in their establishment, the store shut down and turned into an autograph session. Customers and employees alike lined up for the privilege of shaking Jonah's hand and having their pictures taken with the icon. Some even tried to get their tongues around his rap riffs.

At last, Jonah pulled the plug on the celebrity meet-and-greet. "Thanks! 'Preciate the love. But right now, I'm in the market for the flyest jeans in China. Shirts, too. Show me some mad fashion love." He turned to Dan. "What's your size, cuz?"

Dan was astonished. "I can't afford to buy anything in a place like this!"

"I got you covered," Jonah assured him. "When you roll with the Wiz, you've got to look like you roll with the Wiz."

Dan hesitated. Was he being bribed? "I don't know when I'll be able to pay you back," he said cautiously.

"It's all good. Let me do you a solid to make up for the crocs. And when we find your sis, we'll be straight."

When they left the Friendship Shopping Center, Dan was resplendent in designer jeans that cost more than a plasma TV, basketball shoes autographed by Yao Ming, and a limited edition silk-screen T-shirt that the salesman insisted read ROCK DA HOUSE in Chinese.

As they climbed back into the limo, a young girl on

the street asked Dan for his autograph. He was a little ashamed at feeling so pleased.

Jonah grinned like a proud parent. "Now you're getting it," he approved as they drove away. "We'll have you partying like a rock star in no time."

Dan turned to Jonah's father. "Any luck finding Amy and Nellie?"

"They aren't in the major hotels," Broderick Wizard reported. "But don't worry. There are hundreds of smaller inns and guesthouses in and around Beijing. We'll track them down."

Dan gazed out the Hummer's window. Night was falling. He wondered what Amy was doing right now. Was she worried about him? Or did she consider it *his* problem to get back to her, since he'd been the one to storm away?

She's probably still mad. I almost took her head off in Tiananmen Square . . . maybe I should have.

And what about Nellie? Surely the au pair handbook had a rule against leaving one of your charges to wander a Chinese megacity alone.

No one felt like going out for dinner, so the Wizard entourage hired the head chef of the hotel restaurant to come to their penthouse suite and cook for them.

Afterward, they watched pay-per-view movies in the private home theater while Jonah autographed a stack of "Wassup, Yo" publicity photographs.

Dan imagined ecstatic kids all around the world receiving a letter from their hero. "It's really cool that you answer every single fan letter."

Jonah was the image of modesty. "Used to be a time when my concerts didn't sell out in eight minutes, and my show was on basic cable. Paparazzi are the worst, but not half as bad as when nobody wants to take your picture. You do it—for the fans. They gave you what you've got; they can take it away." He tossed a game controller into Dan's hands. "Do you Xbox, cuz?"

"Bring it!" Dan challenged. He hadn't played video games since before Grace's funeral.

Many wounded GIs, slain dragons, vaporized spacecraft, and demolished police cars later, Dan and Jonah hunched over their controllers in the midst of a one-on-one all-night gaming marathon.

Weird, Dan reflected—Jonah Wizard was practically Dan's opposite. Jonah was rich; Dan was flat broke. Jonah was famous; Dan was nobody. Jonah had powerful parents; Dan was an orphan. Jonah was supported by TV and record companies and, from a distance, the entire Janus branch. Dan? He'd never been so completely alone.

And yet playing video games with Jonah was the most normal thing Dan had done since the contest had begun.

"Looks like you're bunking with us tonight," Jonah said, clicking off the Xbox. "We'll find your sis tomorrow."

It brought Dan back to earth with a discordant clunk. "Your dad came up empty?"

"So far," Jonah admitted. "Computers here are all based on Chinese characters. It's tough to know how a hotel clerk is going to spell a name like Cahill or Gomez. The cell phone thing's a killer, man."

"We could still leave a message," Dan suggested hopefully. "They might be able to call in from a pay phone or something."

"Already done," Jonah confirmed. "If your sis is looking for you, she'll know where to track you down."

Dan looked up in surprise. "You don't think she's looking for me?"

"Of course she's looking for you, cuz! That's a definite! You know, probably." The famous eyes scrutinized Dan. "Yo, Pops!" Jonah called to his father. "Hook my man up with a room. Nothing cheap, either. I want a def crib, got it?"

Later, Dan lay in the silk sheets of his very own suite, savoring the taste of the mint he had found on his pillow. *Def* really was the word for it—five-star hotel, designer decoration, sixty-inch plasma screen. It must have cost a fortune, not that Jonah was hurting for money. The one thing it didn't have—

He missed the sound of Amy's breathing. Always just a touch too fast, fueled by the nervous dreams of a world-champion worrywart. Quiet, barely audible. But to her brother, as unmistakable as a police siren.

Amy—was she okay?

If I got kidnapped, she might also be in danger. . . .

And Dan's abduction had been at the hands of Ian

and Natalie. The Kabra *kids* were bad enough, but what if Amy had been visited by their mother? Isabel — the murderer . . .

Don't be such a baby! Everything's fine. You heard Jonah — they'll find Amy tomorrow.

It occurred to Dan that, just as the Kabras had used hired muscle to kidnap him, the Wizards might be using the high life to do exactly the same thing.

But if that's true, why put me in my own room, free to take off any time I want?

He got up, opened the door, and peered both ways down the long hall. No Broderick Wizard watching his suite while texting on his BlackBerry. No record company flunky. He could leave when he pleased — if he had anywhere to go.

Was it really so hard to believe that Jonah actually felt bad about the crocodile thing and was trying to make amends?

"Trust no one," William McIntyre, Grace's lawyer, had told them at the beginning of the contest. Yet Jonah had shown him nothing but kindness today. And the last time Dan had seen Amy, she had bombarded him with hateful accusations about their parents. If anyone deserved not to be trusted, it was her.

For all he knew, she was totally thrilled to be rid of him. She probably hadn't given him a second thought since Tiananmen Square, when he'd turned and walked out of her life.

CHAPTER 8

Amy barely slept a wink.

Worry mingled with jet lag in her mind, a toxic brew that had her watching the LED readout on her bedside clock throughout the long night. Never did more than ten minutes go by between red-eyed updates.

In the other bed, Nellie was also sleeping fitfully, murmuring under her breath through nervous dreams. Even Saladin was restless and had coughed up three fur balls by morning.

It was after five when Amy finally fell into an exhausted sleep. She was plagued by nightmares about her brother wandering through the deserted predawn gloom of Tiananmen Square. He would know no other place to look for her. And where was she? Safe in bed.

It was all her fault. Why had she burdened her brother with her deepest fears about Mom and Dad? No eleven-year-old was ready to face something like that. She wasn't sure she could face it herself.

Nellie's urgent whispering penetrated her reverie. ". . . in Russia they ran ahead of me on purpose. This is different. Dan knew we were in the square, waiting for him, and he didn't come back—"

Amy sat up. "Who are you talking to?"

Startled, Nellie slammed down the hotel phone. "Your uncle Alistair," she said quickly. "We got cut off."

Amy frowned. "No offense, but that's not your call. We don't want to have anything to do with Alistair. He was there the night our parents were killed."

Nellie was stubborn. "That was then and this is now. You're in charge of the clue hunt. But when one of you kids goes missing, that's Nellie time. Do you speak Chinese? Me, neither. We need someone who'll pick up on it if there's a story around town about a lost American boy."

Amy nodded, chastened. "Call him back. Thanks, Nellie."

They arranged to meet Uncle Alistair at the Imperial Hotel in half an hour. And as they slipped out the door, leaving Saladin asleep on a pillow, a tiny nagging doubt tugged at Amy's mind. If Nellie had just been talking to Alistair on the phone, how come she'd had to look up the number?

"Amy. Nellie."

Alistair Oh stood as they approached his table and gallantly saw them into their chairs before reseating himself. He may have been a backstabber like all the other Cahills, but his manners were impeccable.

"I took the liberty of ordering breakfast. Please help yourselves."

Amy and Nellie dug in ravenously. In the tumult of Dan's disappearance, they had skipped dinner.

"Amy, you must be frantic," Alistair said in a mixture of sympathy and worry. "Dan lost in Beijing. All of us who love you will find this most upsetting."

Amy's lips were tight. "How much did you love us when you faked your own death in Korea?"

Uncle Alistair did not apologize. "That was different. A clue was involved. We Cahills are destined to serve two masters—our humanity and the thirty-nine clues."

"And if a clue becomes involved again this time?" Nellie put in pointedly.

"I care deeply about Dan, just as you do," he assured them, his expression pinched. "Where did you last see him?"

"In Tiananmen Square," replied Amy, mangling the name with her full mouth. "Near the Gate of Heavenly Peace. We had an argument, and he ran away and never came back."

The older man was astonished. "But you and your brother are so close. What were you fighting about?"

Amy stuck out her jaw. "The night our parents died. The fire Isabel set. And the other people who might have been there—like *you*."

Uncle Alistair shut his eyes for so long that both girls thought he might have dozed off. When he looked at them again, it was as if his face had been drawn downward by a kind of peculiar gravity.

"If I could travel back in time and change a single hour, that would be the one," he said, his voice husky with emotion. "Two fine lives extinguished, two beautiful children orphaned. What a terrible calamity."

"Calamity!" Amy sat forward. "You talk about it like it was an accident! Isabel burned our house down!"

Alistair winced, as if the effort of recalling were physically painful. "Do you want the truth?"

"I have all the truth I need!" Amy seethed. "She set fire to your house in Java, and now Irina's gone! She did the same thing seven years ago!"

Alistair nodded tragically. "We all knew Isabel's ruthlessness. I should have foreseen that she was capable of murder. Perhaps that is why I've always felt a special responsibility toward you and your brother — and why his disappearance is so distressing to me."

It was not that Amy had nothing to say to this. She simply did not trust herself to speak without falling to pieces, as if the only thing holding her together were her silence.

Nellie put an arm around her. "I know this is big stuff for you, Amy. But right now we have to concentrate on Dan."

"What do you need from me?" Alistair offered.

Nellie pulled a stack of Beijing newspapers out of a large tote bag and dropped them with a thud on the table in front of him. "Look through these. Anything suspicious—lost American kid, young tourist in trouble, boy found sleeping on the subway—that kind of angle. Check radio and TV news, too."

"What about the US Embassy?" Alistair suggested.

"No embassy!" Amy rasped. "At least, not yet. Dan and I are wanted by Social Services! If they run our names through a computer, we're out of the contest."

"The contest," he repeated carefully. "My dear child, far be it from me to use this terrible situation to pressure you to reveal secrets. But if I perhaps knew what you two were working on—"

"Don't you Cahills ever turn it off?" Nellie interrupted angrily. "How stupid do you think we are? We've got a missing kid, and you're gaming it to squeeze information out of us!"

"It's okay," Amy decided. "Dan might follow the clue hunt, hoping to find us that way." From her backpack, she produced the silk sheet from the Forbidden City and spread it out on the table.

Alistair sat forward, stiff with wonder. "Where did you acquire this item? In the Imperial Palace?"

Nellie spoke up. "Just be grateful that you're seeing it at all. What do you know about it?"

The older man was vastly impressed. He pointed to the red signature chop in the bottom corner. "That is without a doubt the personal seal of Puyi himself, the last emperor of China."

"So it's true!" breathed Amy. "The Qing dynasty were Cahills."

Alistair nodded. "That is well known among the Asian branches of our family. It began with Emperor Qian Long, who ascended the throne in 1736. His mother was related to the Janus in Manchuria."

"But Puyi only reigned until he was six," Amy mused. "No way is this the work of a six-year-old."

"He was no longer emperor," Alistair agreed, "but he was permitted to live the emperor's life until he was eighteen. Like his Qing ancestors, he pursued the arts. And, we now know, the thirty-nine clues."

Amy indicated the "equation" of Cahill symbols. "What do you make of this?"

"It seems fairly self-explanatory. The Lucian, Janus, Tomas, and Ekat branches comprise our family."

"But if it's so obvious, why treat it like some huge secret?" Amy persisted.

Alistair avoided her eyes, focusing instead on the Chinese message on the silk. "This part appears to be a poem. It says:

'That which you seek, you hold in your hand,
Fixed forever in birth,
Where the Earth meets the sky.'"

"Well, that explains everything," Nellie said sarcastically, jotting down his translation on a napkin.

"Some poem," scoffed Amy. "It doesn't even rhyme."

The older man regarded her with perplexity. "Surely

you know, Amy, that poetry is often free verse."

"*I* do," Amy replied shakily. "I was just thinking that, if Dan were here, that's what he'd probably say."

It sobered them all.

Uncle Alistair broke the melancholy silence. "To business, then." He scanned the headlines of the *Beijing Daily* and then opened the paper to page two.

A very famous face smirked out at them.

"Jonah Wizard!" Amy exclaimed. "Why is that bonehead getting so much press?"

Alistair scanned the article. "It would appear our Janus rival is also in Beijing. He's performing a rap concert at the Bird's Nest this evening."

"I remember that stadium from the Olympics," Nellie put in. "How's a no-talent creep like him going to fill that place? It holds, like, eighty thousand people."

"And we're going to be two of them," announced Amy.

Nellie made a face. "Why would a missing kid go to a hip-hop concert?"

"Think, Nellie. He doesn't know the language, he's got no money, he can't go to the embassy, he can't find us. Jonah's a familiar face for him."

Alistair frowned. "We're all anxious to find Dan, but this seems far-fetched. It makes very little sense to go."

"Maybe," said Amy. "But it makes even less to stay away."

CHAPTER 9

From backstage, the sound system in the Bird's Nest was shattering. The drumbeats were artillery shells. The capacity crowd swallowed this incoming fire and howled for more—eighty-one thousand people in frenzied overdrive, rattling the interlacing steel "twigs" of the most famous stadium in the world.

Dan had never much appreciated Jonah as a person or as a celebrity. But the guy definitely knew how to work an audience, even a humongous one that didn't speak much English. He conjured his rhymes like Zeus conjured thunderbolts. And yet, when he addressed the crowd in his down-to-earth way, it was somehow intimate, as if every one of the eighty-one thousand were enjoying a personal visit with the megastar. He was electrifying.

Clutching his backstage pass, Dan stood in the wings with Jonah's father and assorted roadies, bodyguards, and music journalists. He couldn't help wondering why Jonah even bothered with the 39 Clues. Who needed to become the most powerful person in history when being famous was so flat-out awesome? Jonah had it all — money, fame, screaming girls. Even the Cahill family had nothing to offer compared with that.

A few feet away, Mr. Wizard's BlackBerry lit up like a Roman candle, and he took an urgent phone call.

Dan looked on eagerly. "Is that about my sister? Have you found their hotel?" He had to cup his hands to his mouth and shout directly into the man's ear.

"No — no luck on that!" Jonah's father yelled back. "But this is an emergency! The fans have broken through to the tunnel outside the dressing room. Security says there are hundreds of them! It's not going to be easy to get Jonah out of here! Come on!"

He led Dan and the bodyguards through a heavy door marked RESTRICTED ACCESS in a dozen languages. Now they were in the true guts of the Bird's Nest, the passages no one got to see during the Olympics on TV. They navigated the network of underground concrete tunnels, squinting in the harsh fluorescent light. After a few turns, they emerged into the main corridor and sheer bedlam.

Five hundred Jonah Wizard fans, amped up to fever pitch, were jammed in like sardines, screaming for a glimpse of their idol. They held up signs, in Chinese and English, with messages like MARRY ME, JONAH; I WANNA BE *YOUR* GANGSTA; and THE YEAR OF THE WIZ. The never-ending chant of *Jo-nah! Jo-nah! Jo-nah!* rivaled the gigawatt sound system of the stadium.

Broderick and the security guards formed a human

wall, holding the fans back, and Dan joined them.

A fistful of Chinese money was thrust into his face by a girl even younger than he was.

"I must meet him! One kiss!" she shrieked. Her face was the color of an overripe tomato, so flushed was she with emotion.

A paper airplane came sailing from the middle of the crowd and bounced off Dan's head. He unfolded it and giggled in amazement. The page contained a pink impression of kissing lips along with a Beijing telephone number.

At that moment, Amy, Nellie, and the Clue hunt might as well have been a million miles away.

Amy and Nellie were less than a hundred feet back, at the edge of the surging crowd.

"You know, this kind of brings back memories," shouted Nellie, straining to push ahead in the sea of people. "Green Day at Fenway Park, summer 2005. I sucker punched a bouncer and got Billie Joe Armstrong to autograph my forehead. I didn't wash my face for a month."

"But how are we going to get through to Jonah to ask if he's seen Dan?" cried Amy in despair. "No way can we sucker punch all these people!"

Suddenly, Jonah's voice echoed through the underground tunnels of the Bird's Nest. *"Good-night, Beijing! You're the bomb! Word!"*

The stadium rocked with cheers. In the corridor, the already charged atmosphere went supercritical. The chanting ceased; the cheering ceased; the signs were dropped. Five hundred crazed fans devoted all their energy to pushing.

At the front, Dan, Broderick Wizard, and the security guards struggled to hold off the advancing wall of humanity. Even Jonah, who saw frenzied admirers everywhere he went, was alarmed by the ferocity of this onslaught.

"Let's get out of here, yo! These people are psycho!"

He wheeled away from the dressing room and sprinted for the emergency exit.

That was when Dan made his first mistake. He took his eye off the crowd and turned to look at Jonah. The girl with the money leaped onto his back and hung on, clamping her arms around his head. Blinded, he staggered backward, and the throng poured in through the opening in the line.

When the crowd began to move, oozing forward like an enormous amoeba, Nellie tucked Amy behind her and plowed into the fray.

Amy followed, stumbling over fallen fans, putting all her faith in the au pair. If Amy had bothered to look down instead of scanning the area for a glimpse of Jonah, she would have seen that she had very nearly stepped on the brother she was so anxious to find.

Nellie and Amy barreled right over Dan, following the stampede.

"Faster!" Amy shouted.

Nellie stopped, poised like a pointer. The herd was thundering down the hallway to Jonah's dressing room. But Nellie's sharp eyes were focused on the emergency exit.

"You think he left the building?" Amy panted.

"You don't get Billie Joe Armstrong's autograph on your forehead without following your instincts," she shot back. "Come on!"

They blasted through the door to see a Hummer stretch limo parked at the curb. The window was down, revealing none other than Jonah Wizard inside, drinking from a water bottle.

A bodyguard jumped out of the front of the car and moved to bar their way. But Jonah called him back. "It's all good, Bruno. The little chick's my cousin."

Amy saw no reason for small talk. "Jonah, have you heard anything from Dan?"

Jonah looked surprised. "Dan, your brother? Why would he be calling me?"

Those simple words were a cannon-shot to Amy's chest. If Nellie had not been there to hold her up, she might have collapsed on the spot.

"Something wrong?" Jonah asked with concern.

Amy tried to answer, but there seemed to be a short circuit between her brain and her mouth. She had pinned so much hope on the idea that Dan had somehow found Jonah. How crazy was that — like a gambler piling his life savings on a single number on a roulette wheel! And now that her bet had come up empty . . .

He's gone . . .

Not temporarily separated or turned around. Lost. For more than twenty-four hours now. A real missing person. And she had absolutely no idea where to look for him.

"We got separated from Dan," Nellie explained to Jonah. "Our cells don't work here, so he's got no way to reach us. We thought he might come to you because you're the most visible."

Jonah nodded. "Makes sense. I'll keep my eyes open. He still might show up."

"Thank you," Amy managed, fighting back tears. "I know we're not on the same side, but Dan's only eleven. This is a *huge* country, and there are"—an image of Isabel Kabra appeared in her mind—"bad people out there. Some things are more important than winning."

"Right—uh—word." The megastar's eyes strayed to the exit. "Can I offer you ladies a ride? You don't want to get busted if the cops call in the riot squad."

He hustled them inside, and the limo drove off. Amy and Nellie were passing through the Bird's Nest VIP gate when the object of their search stepped out of the emergency exit in the company of Jonah's father.

They had missed seeing Dan by fifteen seconds.

The Chinese TV network provided the surgeon who

stitched up the nasty cut over Dan's eyebrow where the money girl had used his face as a starting block for her bull run at the dressing room.

Jonah was contrite. "Sorry, cuz. Never meant for you to end up in the middle of a feeding frenzy. My fault."

Dan tapped the Steri-Strip on his forehead. Regular people sat in the emergency room, getting coughed on and waiting hours to be seen. When you were with the Wizard posse, a private doctor came to your hotel at two in the morning. It made getting stitches almost a luxury experience.

"It's okay," Dan told him. "Thanks for the doctor."

"Least I could do. Listen, we haven't located your sis yet, and this is our last night in Beijing."

"You're leaving?" What was Dan going to do with no Amy *and* no Jonah? Could he make it on his own in this vast alien city?

Jonah nodded. "Places to go, people to see. Here's the thing—I know you can handle yourself, yo. But as your cousin, I can't dump you in Beijing all alone. It's just not cool."

"I have to find Amy."

"True," Jonah agreed. "But look—we both know the real reason we're in China, and it has nothing to do with TV shows or concert tours. The next clue is here somewhere."

If there was one topic Dan wasn't in the mood for, it was the 39 Clues. "So?"

"So even though we're not on the same team, your

sis is looking for the same clue. The way to find her is on the clue hunt."

It wasn't hard to see the truth. Maybe Dan was out of the contest, but Amy was still hot after Clues.

"Come with us, cuz," Jonah went on. "We'll find her together. I got you."

Cold suspicion chilled Dan from the inside. *I quit, but Jonah doesn't know that. To him, I'm still the competition.*

What if this was a trap — a plan to strand Grace Cahill's grandchildren oceans apart from each other? Nile crocodiles were a minor inconvenience compared with losing his sister.

McIntyre's words again: *Trust no one.*

Yeah, real helpful advice — I've got no Amy and no money. If I don't trust somebody, I'm sleeping on the street!

Aloud, he said, "It's pretty risky. If you and Amy are working different angles, we could end up thousands of miles away from each other."

"Word," Jonah agreed seriously. "I'm not going to lie and tell you it can't happen. But you've got a better chance tracking her down on the clue hunt than by hoping to run into her in a city of seventeen million."

"But what if she's looking for me *here*?"

The star shook his head. "Then we would have found her by now. It's not just my pops — we've got the whole Wizard PR machine on this job. No way she's local."

It made sense. Why would Amy waste time waiting around for Dan?

She probably hates me after what happened in Tiananmen Square. . . .

"You're right, Jonah. I'll stay with you guys. Where to next?"

"Change in plan," the star replied. "I was scheduled for a state tour of the Great Wall, but that'll have to wait. Sorry if I can't give you all the details, but this is hardcore inside-baseball Janus info. One day, when you guys figure out which branch you belong to, you'll understand the code of silence they slap on you."

"I understand," Dan said, thinking darkly of his secret Madrigal identity. "I haven't told you everything, either."

"Anyway, we're going to Henan Province to a place called the Shaolin Temple. Heard of it?"

Dan was bug-eyed. "You mean the place where kung fu was developed? Those are the sweetest fighting skills ever!"

"The Janus are all about that," Jonah went on. "You know — martial *arts*? We're more than just pastels and harpsichords."

"This is going to be awesome!" Dan exclaimed. "Is it far? How do we get there?"

"Chinese TV has a private jet we can use. When you roll with me, you go first class."

Alistair Oh was absently doodling on his paper place mat at the dim sum restaurant when Amy and Nellie joined him.

"Nice calligraphy," Nellie commented.

Startled, the older man leaped to his feet, upending his walking stick, which clattered to the floor. "Good morning!" He seated them in his gallant old-world fashion.

"What does it say?" Amy asked listlessly.

"I beg your pardon?"

She indicated the Chinese character on his place mat, elaborately formed despite the fact that he was using a ballpoint pen rather than the customary paintbrush.

"That word. What does it mean?"

"Oh, this. It says—'charm,'" he replied, looking a little uncomfortable. "Never mind that, Amy. Where is your brother?"

"We didn't find him." Amy was working hard to hold it together, but the dark circles around her eyes revealed the depth of her worry. "I'm getting really freaked. What if Isabel Kabra has him?" Isabel, the human worst-case scenario.

"Calm down." Nellie put an arm around her shoulders. "It doesn't help Dan if we panic."

"Isabel is not the problem." Alistair held up a copy of the *Beijing Daily*, featuring a picture of Jonah at the Bird's Nest. "This is what I called you about."

Nellie shook her head sadly. "Old news, Uncle A. Bad music. Good riot. No Dan."

"Jonah's keeping an eye out for him," Amy added. "I know he's the enemy, but I think he really cares."

Alistair was unimpressed. "Allow me to translate." He read from the middle of the article. "'Police broke up the altercation before there were any serious injuries. But one member of the Wizard entourage, Mr. Daniel K. Hill, was treated for a minor cut above his left eye. Mr. Hill, a young cousin of the superstar, described the scene as Ladies' Night Smackdown . . .'"

"He's alive!" Amy exploded. "Who else could think of wrestling at a time like this?"

Nellie's powerful sigh of relief sent paper napkins aloft. "Thank God! He's still lost, but at least he's okay.

I mean, he's with Jonah—" Her face twisted. "That stuck-up tin-plated little hip-hop freak show! I should have known he was lying!"

Alistair clucked wanly. "How little our Janus cousins have changed over time. In the years leading up to the Second World War, Puyi became a Japanese puppet in exchange for the chance to be emperor again—just as Jonah has become so obsessed with his own purposes that he can't see the anguish he's inflicting."

"Or he sees it fine and flat-out doesn't care," the au pair suggested darkly.

Amy struggled to keep her emotions in check. "But why would Jonah kidnap Dan? And more important, why would my idiot brother play along with it?"

"The second question you've answered yourself," Alistair replied. "He has nowhere else to go. He probably believes he's an invited guest. As for Jonah's motive—isn't it obvious? The search for the thirty-nine clues."

Nellie frowned. "He's got money up the wazoo and connections everywhere. What does he need Dan for?"

"Don't you know?" Surprised, Alistair turned from the au pair to Amy. "You children have created quite a stir in the hunt."

"Why?" asked Amy. "We've outsmarted a few people, but I don't think we're winning." She paused. "Are we?"

"Perhaps not, but you're younger than the rest of us, with fewer resources, no branch to support you, and almost zero knowledge of our family history. Many predicted you wouldn't last a week. Yet here you are, right in the thick of things. Maybe you've inherited some of Grace's abilities, or perhaps your outsider status allows you to see the big picture. Whatever it is, Jonah seems to believe it can help him."

"I don't care about the contest," Amy said impatiently. "Not until we've got Dan back. Who knows what Jonah's going to do when he's through with him? They've got crocodiles here, too!"

"At least now we know where to look," Nellie reminded her. "Find Jonah and we've found Dan. One thing about being a world-renowned jerk-face — he can't hide. Wherever he goes, it makes the news."

Alistair scanned the article. "According to this, his next stop is the Great Wall."

"Then so is ours," Amy decided.

"My dear," he told her, "the Great Wall of China is over four thousand miles long. Since Jonah is traveling from Beijing, we can make an educated guess that he will visit the Badaling section, closest to here. But even that is a vast amount of territory to cover."

"Jonah's a celebrity," Amy argued. "If he's there, we'll find him." Her face turned grim. "We have to if we want to save Dan."

Broderick Wizard frowned out the window of the Gulfstream G5. Far below, the rolling Chinese countryside gave way to a wide sprawl of houses and low apartment buildings. "I thought Dengfeng was supposed to be a little village. There's a lot of population down there."

"Welcome to China," the flight attendant told him with a smile. "Even the small towns are big."

"When you've got one-point-three billion people, you have to stick them wherever they fit," suggested Dan from the depths of a forest of sodas, milk shakes, and snacks of all varieties.

It was a good thing Dan took advantage of the extravagance of the jet ride, because the comforts evaporated on the ground. The airport was little more than a landing strip, and their "limo" turned out to be a 1969 Volkswagen Bus.

Their driver spoke no English but kept up an elaborate travelogue in Chinese for the hour-long ride. The first thing Dan noticed in Shaolin was a small strip of souvenir shops and restaurants. Not even this remote corner of Asia could escape tourism. Then he saw it—the fields surrounding the main path were filled with kung fu classes—dozens of teachers and students in the orange robes of the Shaolin monks.

He pressed his face against the fly-specked window of the VW and watched. "How cool is this?"

"Off the chain," Jonah agreed absently.

Dan recognized Jonah's tunnel vision. The star was so focused on the next Clue that he barely noticed his surroundings. He couldn't help wondering if Amy was the same way right now—so engrossed in the hunt that she had barely a thought for her brother.

The driver dropped them off with elaborate instructions no one understood, and they continued on foot.

The first view of the Shaolin Temple was of a magic floating kingdom. Nestled in the Songshan mountain range, the huge complex of hip-roofed structures seemed to float on the clouds.

This was the cradle of martial arts. All at once, Dan understood Amy's excitement when the contest took her to the footsteps of the history she loved so much. Standing between the foo dog statues that guarded the front entrance, he could almost feel the fifteen hundred years of super-sweet fighting skills that had been refined in this very spot.

If Amy were here, she could exact some revenge for the hard time he'd given her at all those museums and research libraries — *oh, the boring Shaolin Temple, boring kung fu, I'm so bored. . . .*

Of course, Amy would never say that stuff. It was Dan who went around affixing the Dan Cahill Seal of Disapproval to anything he deemed uncool. Which was — let's face it — an awful lot.

On the other hand, forget Amy! I'm a Madrigal! We're stone-cold killers! What do we care about family — we probably eat our young —

An image of his parents appeared in his mind, bringing him up short. He didn't remember much about them, but the memories he had were not stone-cold at all. The thought triggered a stab of longing.

A young monk with a shaved head and orange robes

exposing one shoulder stepped in front of Broderick and pointed to the BlackBerry in his hand.

"Photography forbidden," he said with a heavy accent.

"I'm not going to take any pictures," Jonah's father promised airily.

Like lightning, the monk snatched the device out of his hand. "Return camera later."

Dan had never seen a human move that fast before.

Jonah's father was outraged. "That's my lifeline to the world!"

"It's all good, Pops," soothed his son. "Give the thumbs a rest."

As they passed through the gate, the monk gave each member of the Wizard party a thorough once-over, especially Jonah.

They probably don't get a lot of hip-hop kids in Henan Province, Dan reflected.

Soon they found themselves in the Chang Zhu court-yard, surrounded by sculptures and frescoes. Dan was fascinated. Most of the art depicted fighting figures in every imaginable kung fu pose.

From there, they entered the Hall of One Thousand Buddhas, with its central shrine of bronze and white jade.

"Notice the floor is uneven," intoned a monk guiding a group of British tourists. "These depressions come from long-term foot-stamping practices of Shaolin teachers with profound kung fu powers."

Dan made it a point to step in one. He could almost feel the energy.

Although there were no stairs, the farther they moved through the series of halls, the higher they seemed to climb. The temple was built directly into the mountainside and moved up with the slope.

Jonah's father regarded the thick stone walls covered in frescoes of martial arts scenes. "No way would I get reception in here anyway."

The largest crowd of visitors was gathered around an exhibit protected by a Plexiglas case. "This is the shadow stone, the most sacred artifact in the temple," another Shaolin guide was explaining to his tour group. "The fifth-century monk Bodhidharma sat facing this rock for nine years of silent meditation. When his eyes began to close out of weariness, he tore his own eyelids off. He maintained the lotus position for so long that his legs withered away. And the sun was so strong that his shadow was cast onto this stone with such detail that even the pleats of his clothing can be seen."

No wonder the Shaolin are tough, thought Dan. He wasn't a big fan of meditation, and definitely not the eyelids part. But talk about willpower! What a fighter this Bodhidharma guy must have been — when he had legs, of course.

Jonah let out a snicker. "I guess homey wasn't much for winking and tap-dancing after that."

The guide regarded him with scorn. "Rude jokes are not welcome here. Bodhidharma is the monk who brought Zen Buddhism to China and introduced the art of kung fu to the Shaolin Temple."

"Chill." Jonah held up his arms in a gesture of innocence. "No need to go medieval on the Gangsta—"

"'Gangsta'?" Suddenly, the monk's eyes widened in wonder, and he called out in agitated Mandarin.

Monks came running from throughout the building, converging on the Shadow Stone.

Jonah's cocky sneer vanished. "Whoa, I was just playing around! I didn't mean no disrespect!"

His father reached into his BlackBerry belt holder, but there was nothing there to dial for help on.

Even Dan was nervous as he watched the orange robes congregate around them, a collection of kung fu masters capable of unleashing unimaginable martial arts force.

"Word!" Jonah was babbling now. "I'm down with the respect thing! I'm all about respect for—uh—great traditions and—uh—orange dresses—"

The monks continued to assemble, their piercing stares burning into Jonah. At last, an older monk who seemed to be in charge said, "So it is true, yes? You are Jonah Wizard, the American television and music performer?"

CHAPTER 11

Never before had the famous Jonah Wizard felt so lost at sea. He could usually charm his way out of any situation. But his patented hip-hop charisma didn't work on Shaolin monks.

Dan scanned the temple for the nearest exit. They were badly outnumbered by trained martial arts masters. Escape would be their sole option if this got ugly.

The head monk went on. "You have many admirers among our order, Jonah Wizard. We find similarities between our ritual chants and your—I believe the term is 'hip-hop groove'? We consider you to be, as you might say, 'all that.'"

Jonah laughed with pure relief. "Thanks, yo. Nice to be kickin' it in—you know—wherever we are."

"I am Li Wu Chen, Chief Abbot of the Shaolin Order," the man introduced himself. "Please honor us by coming this way."

The procession of monks led them farther into the temple. Jonah walked beside the abbot, with Broderick and Dan bringing up the rear. They passed through room after room of Chinese art treasures that rivaled the Palace Museum in the Forbidden City. Farther on, the library hall featured countless shelves of ancient manuscripts. At last, they stepped through an elaborately carved archway. Dan felt the temperature drop, and he understood that they were no longer in the building on the mountainside but inside the mountain itself. There were no tourists here, no souvenir stands, no signs in a dozen languages. This was the heart of the Shaolin Temple, a secret place reserved for only a handful of chosen visitors.

Dan peered into a huge chamber where several monks — obviously the top fighters — were engaged in a spectacular battle. The movements were so fast, yet so perfectly fluid and natural, that at first glance, the lightning combat seemed almost like dance. But this was no ballet. The punches and kicks cut the air like bullets, leaving whispers of sound. Bodies soared, as if gravity did not exist. Watching it, Dan realized that all the martial arts he had seen in the fields of Shaolin had been child's play by comparison.

It took him several seconds to find his voice. Still, it was in a hushed whisper that he said, "This is the coolest kung fu I've ever seen in my life!"

Li Wu Chen smiled tolerantly. "We prefer to call it *wushu* here. The word *kung fu* can mean any skill mastered through long practice. *Wushu* refers specifically to martial arts. Would the young man care for a lesson?"

Dan's heart very nearly blasted through his rib cage and leaped out of his chest. "Me? With these guys? You're kidding!"

"There is no kidding in the Shaolin order," the abbot deadpanned. "But if you wish, we will show you a few of the fine points."

"Oh, I wish!" Dan exclaimed fervently. "I wish!"

The bus ride to the Great Wall was scheduled for seventy minutes, but that obviously didn't include Beijing traffic. At the seventy-minute mark of their trip, Amy and Nellie were still gridlocked on the freeway, and they were having a hard time restraining Saladin. The Egyptian Mau was expressing more than average interest in the plump hen in the arms of a peasant farmer in the next row.

"I feel sorry for that chicken," Nellie commented. "Her options are lousy — the tender mercies of Saladin, or the stew pot of that family. Either way, the end of her day is going to be a bummer."

Amy was deep in the pages of *Puyi: The Last Son of Heaven*, a thick paperback she had picked up at the bus station bookshop. But her mind was never far from her brother. "Is anybody wearing a Jonah Wizard T-shirt?" she asked, scanning the aisle. "If we find a real fan, maybe we can follow him to Jonah — and Dan."

"I don't think this is the fan bus," Nellie observed glumly. "More like the poultry bus."

In fact, Nellie had been checking for T-shirts — and

hats, belt buckles, Pez dispensers, and authentic Wizard Enterprises Bling™ ever since the Beijing terminal. She had even been sidling up to random teenagers in hip-hop clothing, hoping to pick up snippets of Jonah's music on their iPods. No luck.

How could they have lost Dan? If Amy was frantic about finding her brother, Nellie was doubly so. She was outwardly calm—no point in making Amy even more distraught. But these were *her* kids—in *her* care—and one of them was missing!

Well, not missing, technically. Dan was with Jonah, which was better than him vanishing completely or landing in the clutches of Isabel Kabra. Jonah wasn't the worst of those Cahill vipers, but that was like saying it was preferable to be attacked by a tiger shark than a great white. Especially since Jonah was up to something. Why else would he lie to them about Dan?

Nellie's instructions were clear: "Finding Dan is important," the voice on the other end of the crackly line had told her. "But *nothing* takes precedence over the clue hunt."

"You're talking about an eleven-year-old kid!" Nellie had shouted into the pay phone.

"Who happens to be Grace Cahill's grandson," the voice had added. "He has shown himself to be quite a resourceful young man. We have every reason to believe he can take care of himself."

Big talk from someone sitting in a paneled office thousands of miles away.

Suddenly, the pressure of keeping her real mission a secret seemed nearly as exhausting as the Clue hunt. Nellie slumped in her seat, hugging Saladin to her chest.

The guilt gave her no respite. These poor kids had been deceived practically from birth — first by their parents, who had hid their Cahill identity, then by Grace, who had withheld the truth about the fire. Next, the Clue hunt — practically a double-crossers' convention. Who knew what lies Jonah was telling Dan right now?

And on top of it all, there's me — someone they trust. Someone who's supposed to protect them . . .

If it ever came down to a choice between the mission or Amy and Dan —

Don't get ahead of yourself. Worry about today's problems, not what might happen tomorrow. Find Dan. Keep Amy from losing it —

After all, whatever Nellie's covert role, she was still an au pair. The kids were her responsibility. That included Dan's safety *and* Amy's mental health.

Keep her distracted.

She turned to Amy. "How's the book? Any leads?"

Amy shrugged. "Puyi was a Janus, all right. I recognize the type — spoiled rotten, nuts about art, totally self-centered. According to this, his life was basically one extended hissy fit after he was kicked off the throne. It wasn't so bad while they let him stay in the Imperial Palace. He still had eunuchs to worship him and servants to do his bidding. When he demanded a Western education, they brought him a tutor all the way from London. He loved the West—even took an English name: Henry."

"Emperor Henry," Nellie mused. "Has a nice ring to it. Like King Ralph."

"When they threw him out of the Forbidden City, he kind of fell apart. He turned into a real playboy, a do-nothing rich guy. Sound like anybody we know?"

"At least Jonah raps for a living," Nellie offered. "I mean, he's a world-class idiot, but he has a job."

There was a roar as the bus picked up speed. They were moving again.

"During World War Two," Amy went on, "the Japanese set Puyi up as emperor of Manchukuo—the old Manchuria, where the Qing dynasty had originated. He knew he was just a puppet for Japan, but he needed to feel like a king again. He paid the price, too—when the war was over, he served ten years in jail for it. And after they let him out, he spent the rest of his life as an ordinary citizen working in a library. He died in 1967."

"That's cold," Nellie agreed. "It's a big come-down from jewel-encrusted golden robes. Poor guy peaked at six."

"It's pretty Cahill, too," Amy pointed out bitterly. "They dump everything on your shoulders when you're just a kid. In our family, you don't get a childhood. We're too busy trying to dominate the world."

And I'm a part of that, Nellie reflected as the bus rattled over a pothole. *Pushing children into a lethal game.*

She felt a sudden yearning to take the girl in her arms, to reassure her that everything would be okay, that she'd get to be a normal teenager one day. *Yet that would be deception, too.*

Aloud, she said, "So when Puyi painted that silk and hid it in the secret attic, it had to be *before* he got booted from the Forbidden City. They wouldn't have let him back in and given him the run of the place."

Amy checked the time line at the front of the book. "That happened in 1924, when he was eighteen. Maybe Puyi sensed that his days were numbered in the Imperial Palace, and that's why he wrote the poem." She recited from memory:

"'That which you seek, you hold in your hand,
Fixed forever in birth,
Where the Earth meets the sky.'"

Her brow furrowed. "But what did he *mean*?"

Nellie rolled her eyes. "What do you Cahills ever mean? More thirty-nine clues mumbo jumbo."

Amy frowned. "What *you hold in your hand* can only be the page itself. And it's *not* what we seek, since the clue is someplace else. *Fixed forever in birth* — well, nothing stays exactly the way it is the instant it's born. And *where the Earth meets the sky —*"

"I've got news for you," the au pair said sourly. "The

Earth meets the sky *everywhere.* That's how it works. Earth stops; sky starts. Face it, we've got nothing."

Amy raised an eyebrow. "We don't know what Puyi was trying to say. But we do know when he said it — 1924."

"So?"

Amy pulled Dan's laptop computer from his backpack and powered it on. "So if we research major world events from the early nineteen twenties, we might be able to learn what Puyi was up to. One thing about Cahills — we make the news."

Nellie was skeptical. "The guy went from child emperor to rich slacker, to Japanese puppet, to war criminal, to librarian. What do you expect to find that isn't in the history books?"

"The Cahill connection," Amy explained. "Look, books say Amelia Earhart was trying to fly around the world. *We* know she was really following the clue hunt. I'll bet there's something similar about Puyi."

"Such as?"

On the laptop's encyclopedia, Amy set the yearbook function to 1924. "Okay, within a few months of the day Puyi was exiled, IBM was formed, Joseph Stalin came to power in Russia —"

Not for the first time, Nellie was amazed at the brilliance of the girl's logic. She peered over her shoulder at the screen. "Greece became a republic — ooh, I'd love to go there. The islands, the baklava . . ."

Her voice trailed off as the bus crested a ridge. For

the past half hour, the terrain had been growing hillier, the rises steeper. Suddenly, it was laid out before them — the Great Wall of China.

Beside her, Amy gasped. The ancient barrier stretched up slopes and into valleys, farther than the eye could see in both directions. *Four thousand miles,* Nellie reflected — *long enough to go from Boston to San Diego, and then hang a left to Mexico City.*

"I've seen pictures," Amy said in awe, "but the real thing —"

Even Saladin turned his attention from the chicken in the next row to gaze out the window at the giant structure that loomed up as the bus approached.

Nellie took the computer from Amy's lap and browsed to the Great Wall, glancing back and forth from the pictures on-screen to the mind-blowing reality. The only man-made structure that could be seen from outer space. Once guarded by more than a million men.

During construction, when a worker died, his body was built right into the Wall itself. No one knew how many corpses lay within the stone and mortar, but some estimates ran as high as three million souls.

It was a sight without equal anywhere in the world — unique because of its age, its historical importance, and mostly its unimaginable length.

Nellie's heart sank. To find a single person in such a place — even a celebrity like Jonah Wizard — would be like searching the universe for a grain of sand.

CHAPTER 12

The orange robe looked somehow *right* on Dan—like he was meant to wear it.

"Can somebody take my picture?" He had his collection in mind. This would be the prized piece. He'd have it blown up to twenty feet wide. It would be an entire wall of his trophy room.

"Photography forbidden."

Dan was crushed. He opened his mouth to protest, then thought better of it. You didn't argue with a guy who could rip your arm out and beat you to death with the bloody end. "Can I at least keep the suit?"

His sparring partners smiled tolerantly.

The lesson began. Dan had envisioned himself flying through the air with the greatest of ease. But he was not surprised that it didn't happen that way. As a beginner, he started at the beginning—simple punches and kicks, and learning how to fall.

It doesn't get any better than this, he reflected, slapping the mat in a break-fall. *Learning kung fu—wushu—in a secret part of the Shaolin Temple in the very heart of Mount Song.*

Soon they progressed to basic throws. Dan glowed when the monks praised his balance. And thanks to his extraordinary memory, he was a quick study, with perfect recall of everything he'd been taught.

The highlight of the hour was a sparring session — Dan versus four of the most dangerous fighters in the world. Oh, sure, he knew they were letting him win. But the feeling of throwing a kung fu master was indescribable — even if the guy was mostly throwing himself.

All at once, Dan saw an opening. The monk in front of him was down, perfectly positioned for one of the holds Dan had just learned. This was it — a once-in-a-lifetime opportunity for a novice to star in real Shaolin competition.

As Dan pounced, two powerful hands reached up and grabbed the front of his robe. Suddenly, his opponent's foot was against his abdomen — not kicking, but launching Dan up and over him with astonishing force. Flying through the air, the triumphant thought flashed through his mind: *I just got schooled by a Shaolin master!* It never occurred to him that he was about to break every bone in his body.

The other three caught him and set him gently down on the mat. He did a quick self-inventory — two arms, two legs, everything still attached.

A colossal grin split his face. "That was *mad awesome*! How did you do that?"

His teachers looked vaguely pleased.

"This is the basis of all defense in wushu," the

thrower explained. "The momentum of your adversary is your greatest ally."

Another monk arrived with a tea service and a platter of food, and the sparring was adjourned. Dan bit down on a deep-fried snack and chewed thoughtfully, trying to place the unfamiliar flavor. Not bad, he decided. Crispy, kind of salty — a little like pork rinds, but the texture was different.

"What are these?" Dan asked, popping another piece into his mouth.

"It is a delicacy made from the larva of the silkworm," came the reply.

Dan nearly spit the morsel clear across the room. "We're eating *worms*?"

"No. The silkworm is the caterpillar of the *Bombyx mori* — the silk moth."

Like that was any better. Not worms, bugs. The effort to swallow required all the willpower he could muster. He knew he was imagining it, but he felt an entire insect zoo in his stomach, writhing and buzzing.

He struggled to unsteady feet. "I think I need some air."

One of the monks escorted him through the many twists and turns that led to the Chang Zhu courtyard. He murmured his thanks and staggered out onto the grounds.

I'd never make it as a Shaolin monk. Great martial arts — but the meal plan!

Tourists and visitors regarded him quizically — a Western boy in Shaolin robes. He was too nauseated to be impressed by the sights, but just walking helped to settle his stomach. Jonah was nowhere to be seen. The star was probably still inside the temple, signing autographs for his Shaolin fans.

Dan surveyed his surroundings. What was that? From a distance it looked like a miniature city. He drifted over and discovered that the structures were not buildings but towering brick-and-stone grave markers, shaped like Chinese pagodas, some of them thirty or forty feet tall. A sign declared that this burial ground was the Pagoda Forest — the final resting place for the cremated remains of centuries of Shaolin monks.

Pretty cool — unless you're trying to digest a couple of Bombyx mori*s.*

Just outside the temple grounds, by the side of the road, he noticed a line of coin-operated telescopes trained up Mount Song.

He left the Pagoda Forest and trudged along the path, fishing in his pocket for change. Another advantage of being part of the Wizard posse — Jonah had provided him with some Chinese money.

Exiting via a rear gate, he approached the line of telescopes. He squinted up at the mist-drenched summit of Mount Song. He could make out a distant monument, white against the gray sky. "What is it?"

An attendant supplied the answer. "It is the statue of Bodhidharma."

"You mean the eyelids dude?" Dan blurted.

The man pointed to the money slot. "One yuan."

Dan inserted a coin, and the telescope whirred to life with the ticking of a timer. He peered into the eyepiece.

The statue was carved from white stone — a bearded monk sitting cross-legged atop a brick pedestal. As far as Dan could tell, there were no missing eyelids, and the figure's lower body, shriveled or not, was hidden by robes.

But that wasn't what made Dan gasp.

I know that guy!

Where would a Boston orphan have seen a statue that sat atop a remote Chinese mountain? On TV? The Internet? In a textbook at school?

He had a murky vision of the white sculpture surrounded by thick gray fur . . .

Cat fur . . .

Saladin?

Of course! Grace had kept a small replica of this statue on the landing of her stairs! It had been one of Saladin's favorite spots — the Egyptian Mau used to circle it endlessly, rubbing against the contours of the porcelain.

Amy and Dan had called it the Beard Buddha.

How could I ever forget that thing? I was scared to death of it!

And now he was staring at the real one.

He frowned. They never knew it when she was alive, but Grace Cahill had been embroiled up to her nostrils in the 39 Clues. The entire contest was her creation, written into her will with the help of William McIntyre. A lot of things Grace had casually mentioned over the years had turned out to be vital to the Clue hunt. It was almost like she was still searching from the grave.

He felt a brief flash of irritation at his grandmother. She had implanted so many things like this in his head — and even more in Amy's, since the two of them had been extra close. Sometimes he couldn't escape the feeling that his brain was a computer hard drive infected with dozens of viruses just waiting for some outside trigger to set them off.

The one possibility Grace had never considered was that he might quit the contest and be stuck with all these mental time bombs to drive him crazy. Because, Clue hunt or not, he couldn't help being curious.

1) Jonah's Janus connections had sent him to the Shaolin Temple.

2) That was the *real* Beard Buddha up there.

Coincidence?

Yeah, right.

The white statue loomed high above, seemingly miles in the sky. Directly in front of Dan, an endless series of ancient crumbling stone steps led up the mountain.

A million stairs — at least it looked like that many.

Good thing I ate my silkworm today. . . .

He was going to need the energy.

CHAPTER 13

"That's pretty wild, you guys being fans, yo," Jonah said to Li Wu Chen.

The abbot regarded him disapprovingly. "So long we have waited and the branch sends us a foolish boy."

"Branch?" Jonah repeated. He dropped his voice to a murmur. "You mean—*Janus*?"

"We are not fans of your obnoxious noise. Yes, we are Janus—the one true line of the Cahill family in Asia. We welcome you as the son of Cora Wizard." Li Wu Chen's gaze moved to Jonah's father. "And of course, her non–Janus husband."

It was as if a curtain had been swept aside. No wonder the branch leadership in Venice had sent Jonah here! As Janus representatives, the Shaolin monks might be able to help with a Clue in this part of the world.

"She's got a real sense of humor, my wife," Broderick mumbled, a little resentfully. His thumbs twitched as if his hands felt empty with no BlackBerry in them. "She could have told us the natives were Janus friendlies."

"Chill, Pops," soothed his son. "She got us where

we needed to be, no harm done." Classic Cora Wizard. She ran the branch like one of her performance-art pieces — equipping the actors with limited information and then stepping back to watch the sparks fly. It was very Janus, although he'd never expected her to do it with her own son.

The abbot ushered them into a small antechamber furnished with a rough-hewn round table. The door closed with a sucking sound, and they realized they were in a secure room.

"First things first," Li Wu Chen announced. "Who is the boy, and why is he with you?"

"His name is Dan Cahill," Jonah's father replied.

"Cahill." The abbot sat forward. "Janus?"

Jonah shrugged. "Nobody knows. He's Grace Cahill's grandson."

Li Wu Chen was impressed. "Ah, Grace Cahill. Good bloodlines. Dangerous woman. Few have come as close as she to solving the thirty-nine mysteries that cannot be solved."

"Easy on the lovefest," said Jonah firmly. "Grace did her thing, but my mom's got her smoked. I think that's why Cora hooked us up. Venice is one ingredient shy of duplicating the Janus formula."

The abbot leaped to his feet, shouting something in excited Mandarin. "Please excuse my exuberance," he added sheepishly, reseating himself. "Too long have we Janus in Asia lived in the shadow of those Tomas louts with their large muscles and small minds."

"Word," agreed Jonah, thinking of the Holts.

"Consider the resources of the Shaolin order completely at your disposal. What is the missing ingredient?"

"I'm on it," Jonah assured him. "Mom's convinced it's here in China, but we don't know what it is or where to find it. That's why we're hanging on to the Cahill kid."

Li Wu Chen frowned. "Surely this small boy has no knowledge beyond the grasp of the Janus branch."

"Don't sell the kid short," Jonah insisted. "He looks dumb, but he and his sis have pulled off a lot of miracles. Maybe it's the Grace connection, who knows?"

"Wise to cover all possibilities," the abbot admitted grudgingly. "Perhaps representing the Janus and appearing on the cover of *Tiger Beat* are not mutually exclusive endeavors. Manipulated cleverly, Grace's descendant could prove to be a valuable asset."

"Uh — thanks." Was that supposed to be a compliment?

"Your mother has good reason to search for the missing ingredient in China," Li Wu Chen told him. "Replicating the Janus serum has been the goal of the Qing emperors dating back hundreds of years. It was this obsession — not their admirable devotion to the arts — that caused them to neglect their people."

"But did they get the job done?" Jonah probed. "Did any of those emperors score the formula?"

"We believe the answer is yes."

Broderick spoke up. "Believe? Don't you know?"

The abbot supplied the answer to Jonah, not his

father. "As passed down through the decades, the story is thus: Puyi, the last emperor, hired a tutor named Reginald Fleming Johnston, a Janus scientist from the British Isles. Together, they completed the serum in a secret laboratory in the Forbidden City."

Jonah could tell from his father's scowl that Pops didn't appreciate being ignored. But this was more important than Broderick's bruised ego. "So, what happened to it?" he asked urgently.

"It was most unfortunate. The year was 1924. Puyi sensed that he would soon be exiled. Naturally, the safety of the serum was his paramount concern. Johnston knew a fellow British Cahill with a unique skill that enabled him to hide the formula where it would be preserved indefinitely. It is said that not another man alive at the time could have performed the task."

"But where did he hide it?" Broderick demanded, almost shouting.

Li Wu Chen shook his head. "There the legend ends."

"Tell me about this big player they hired to stash the merchandise," Jonah persisted. "Who was he?"

"This too is not known. After leaving the Forbidden City, Puyi became inactive. Some say he journeyed to the Great Wall prior to his death, but this has never been confirmed. Completing the Janus formula was his one great achievement. Not even his brief reign on the Throne of Heaven could compare. The rest of the life of Henry Puyi—as a figurehead, a prisoner, a simple library clerk—this was no fate for a Janus." The abbot's eyes flashed to Jonah's father before settling back on the star. "For an ordinary person, perhaps even for an emperor. But not for a descendant of Jane Cahill."

With a whoosh, the door to the chamber swept open and in rushed another monk in a state of high anxiety. He held Broderick's BlackBerry between his thumb and forefinger, as if expecting it to explode at any second. The smartphone was lit up like a Christmas tree.

Jonah's father leaped to his feet. "That's Janus business — highest priority code!"

The agitated monk could not have been happier to hand it over and make his escape.

Only when the security door had slurped shut again did Jonah ask, "Is it from Mom?"

His father frowned. "No, not your mother." He held it up. Chinese characters filled the small screen.

Li Wu Chen produced a pair of reading glasses. "Most curious. It is a series of numbers. One, thirty-eight, fifty-three."

Broderick Wizard grimaced. "The message is from a dummy server. It won't let me identify the sender." He thumbed the keypad in frustration. "What's the point of encrypting a meaningless message?"

"Because it's not meaningless, Pops." Jonah was triumphant. "Section one, row thirty-eight, seat fifty-three — yo, this message is a seat location in a stadium!"

"But we don't have any more concerts scheduled this month," his father reminded him.

"Maybe that's the point," the star argued. "We set

up a gig — in Shanghai, let's say — and whoever sent that message knows to show up in that seat. All we have to do is put an agent in the next spot over."

"Risky," Broderick mused.

"Not really. I'll be onstage with a microphone in my hand. If things get really hairy, I can bring fifty thousand screaming fans down on this guy. Even the Lucians don't have that kind of backup." He grinned with all thirty-two perfect teeth. He would have loved to have this get back to Mom somehow.

"Most clever, star of *Who Wants to Be a Gangsta?*" Li Wu Chen told him. "But, alas, you are wrong."

Jonah was insulted. "You're trippin'!"

The abbot regarded him disapprovingly. "Shaolin monks do not 'trip.'"

"No disrespect," Jonah said quickly. "It's just — well, you tell me what that message is supposed to mean."

"Gladly," the abbot agreed. "Are you familiar with the terracotta army at the tombs of Xian?"

Broderick frowned. "The message is from the army?"

"It is not a real army," Li Wu Chen explained with a weary sigh. "The terracotta warriors are considered the eighth wonder of the ancient world. If you could step back from your son's silly career for a moment, you might acquire a measure of wisdom beyond *Entertainment Tonight*."

"Let's all take it down a notch," Jonah suggested, seeing his father redden. The last thing he needed was for Pops to get into a scrap with a Shaolin martial arts master. First of all, Li Wu Chen, although small and slight, could probably lay waste to a city. And second, if Mom found out, the payback would be a monster.

He turned to the abbot. "We didn't mean to dis your ancient wonder. We respectfully ask"— respect was big here — "for the lowdown on this fly army."

"Just outside the city of Xian lies the tomb of Qin Shi Huang, first emperor of a united China. It is defended by a vast buried army of terracotta warrior statues."

"That's it?" asked Jonah. "Statues?"

"They are thousands in number, greater than life-size and carved with spectacular attention to detail. Even now, undiscovered battalions are being unearthed every month."

Jonah's father was skeptical. "But why are you so sure the message is about this place?"

"It is a reference to a specific terracotta figure," Li Wu Chen explained. "The fifty-third soldier in the thirty-eighth rank of the first excavation pit."

"Or," Broderick added, "it could be a trap."

"It's all good," Jonah said blithely. "Trap, no trap, I've got it covered."

The monk was wide-eyed. "Surely even you cannot be so reckless! The son of Cora Wizard would be a fine prize for our rival branches."

Jonah was unruffled. "Won't be me out there on the firing line." A flash of the grin that had graced so many magazine covers. "I knew it would come in handy keeping the Cahill kid around."

CHAPTER 14

After the first three hundred stairs, Dan was breathing hard. By five hundred, he was ready to cough up his lungs and leave them on the flank of Mount Song.

A few times, orange-robed monks and kung fu students puffed past, running up the endless steps. No wonder the Shaolin fighters were unbeatable. If they trained *here*, they could probably bench-press the temple, and maybe the whole mountain with it.

He lost count somewhere around seven hundred fifty, and the Bodhidharma statue was still nowhere to be seen. Perspiration dripped from every pore of his body.

I'm turning my precious wushu outfit into sweat rags!

Dan glanced at his watch—he'd been climbing for nearly an hour. Where was the Beard Buddha—on the moon?

Another group of monks jogged past, this time on the way down. There was a distinct chill in the air now. Surely he was near the top.

The stairs twisted abruptly to the right, and there towered his childhood nightmare, twenty feet tall. An involuntary yelp escaped him. He looked around in embarrassment. No training monks, no wandering tourists. He was alone.

He examined the huge base and then let his eyes wander up the folds of Bodhidharma's robes. There were no markings or symbols — not even a crack in the stone where a secret message might be hidden.

Was I wrong about the Beard Buddha?

As he circled Bodhidharma's bulk, his eyes fell on a small shrine constructed behind the statue. He stepped inside. Chinese writing was everywhere, but a lone sign in English read: DHARMA HOLE. An arrow pointed to an opening in the stone.

A cave!

Oh, how he didn't want to go inside. In the course of the Clue hunt, he'd been in enough tunnels, shafts, pits, and catacombs to last a lifetime. And in some of them, it had very nearly come to that.

But he hadn't climbed that stairway to heaven for nothing. He got down on all fours and crawled inside. It was dark and tight, the rock cold and damp from the misty air.

About fifteen feet in, the cave faded to utter blackness. The shut-in feeling was unendurable — ancient stone pressing on all sides, zero vision. It was as if he'd been swallowed by Mount Song. He began to hyperventilate. Asthma? No, the gasping breaths were bringing air into his lungs, but they were accelerating, and he was powerless to control them.

What was happening to him? Was he sick?

I'm having a claustrophobia attack!

He shut his eyes and tried to pump all thought out of his mind. He was *not* wedged into an unimaginably tight seam inside millions of tons of solid rock. He was just — chilling.

It was only about thirty seconds, but it seemed like an eternity. At last, he was breathing normally and ready to press on.

His probing hand struck a loose rock, and he felt a vibration in his palm. A second later, his knee rattled over the same spot. Odd. He reversed a few inches and tapped at the stone. It made a peculiar sound, not hollow, exactly, but — different.

If only I had a flashlight!

All at once, he realized that he *did* have a light. Not a very bright one, but better than nothing. He aimed his left wrist at the loose piece and pressed the small button that lit up the dial of his watch.

The glow was dim, but it revealed an amazing sight. This stone was not native to the cave. An examination of the edges showed that it had been specially shaped to fit into that very spot.

He scrabbled with his fingers and managed to pry one corner up. It lifted easily. He set it aside and activated the watch light once again.

The exhilaration of discovery flooded over him. He was looking into a secret compartment carved into the rock, not seen by human eyes for who knew how long.

He leaned closer. There lay the tattered remains of a moldy blanket wrapped around—what?

He drew the parcel out and tried to unwrap it. It was no use. This was a two-hand project, impossible to accomplish when one hand was occupied with lighting up the watch face. He reverted to darkness and replaced the stone over the empty compartment. Then he grasped the bundle in his arms and began the arduous journey, inch by inch, reversing out of the cave. Slowly, the light returned, and he was in the open again.

A quick scan of the shrine and the area around the statue. He was still alone. Eagerly, he unwrapped the ancient fabric and examined the contents. His brow knit.

Garbage. Literally! Pots and cups, broken glass, all scorched black and half melted.

Who takes out the trash and hides it like it's something precious and top secret?

He regarded the pieces. Those weren't cups, they were beakers. And the taller, thin ones—broken test tubes and maybe glass pipes. Those were clamps, the screws charred black. This wasn't trash—it was lab equipment! And something had obviously gone very wrong, because the stuff was all burned.

A fire. Wasn't that the Cahill way! His parents, Grace's home, cousin Irina barely a week ago. He could still see her as she fell, as the flaming beach house caved in around her. It was a terrible image—one that had returned to him, unbidden, over and over again since that awful night.

Dan had witnessed a lot since Grace's funeral. But that was the first time he'd ever watched someone die. He remembered Irina's face and couldn't help but wonder if his parents had looked like that when their final moment had come.

No — can't think about that. . . .

His mind traveled back to the underground chamber in Paris. The mural of Gideon Cahill and his four children — Luke, Jane, Thomas, and Catherine — the forebears of the Cahill branches. That picture had showed a fire, too.

Gingerly, he picked up a scorched shard between his thumb and forefinger. The glass was thick and bubbly — barely translucent. The other components were oversize and clunky. They seemed to be made of heavy iron rather than stainless steel or aluminum. How stone-age was this stuff?

His heart began to beat at double speed. Wait a minute! Gideon Cahill had been an alchemist! Could this be the stuff from *his lab* — burned by the very same fire that was depicted in that painting? Henan Province was nowhere near Europe, but five hundred years was a long time, and, let's face it, Cahills got around.

He began to sift through the burned remnants, searching for some hint as to why this debris was so important that it had to be dragged halfway around the world and then hidden.

Ow! A shard pierced his skin, and he sucked on the

bleeding finger. He could almost hear Amy's voice: *I told you not to play with broken glass.*

Oh, yeah? he retorted mentally. *Well I'm the one who found it, not you. And I'm not even part of the clue hunt anymore!*

Looking down from the heights, he spotted the observation platform far below. Two figures the size of ants were crouched at one of the telescopes. Jonah and his dad? He couldn't tell. But they would probably be looking for him about now.

His first instinct was to hide the remains of Gideon's lab. It didn't seem to hold any Clue, but the fact that someone had gone to such great lengths to bring it here meant it was probably important. You didn't hand stuff over to the Janus just like that.

He began to wrap up the pieces. Something tumbled through a rip in the blanket and landed with a clunk at his feet. He reached down and picked it up. It didn't look like part of the lab. It was oval in shape, probably gold — it was hard to tell because it was so blackened. But it had a button catch. He pressed it and the oval popped open.

The inside was lined with what had probably been purple velvet. Nestled there was an ivory miniature, ornately framed and painted with incredible detail.

Dan stared at the face of the young woman portrayed there.

It was his mother!

No, not possible. This stuff is hundreds of years old!

Her hair and her clothes were all wrong—from another time. This couldn't be Hope Cahill.

But it's her face!

Dan had been only four when she'd died. Yet you didn't forget your mother's face. Not ever.

He heard distant voices, chanting in unison. More monks, training on the stairs. He only had a few short moments to hide the lab components—

He regarded the miniature again. But not this. This was staying with him.

He stuck the portrait in the waistband of his underwear, hefted the blanket bundle, and started down the steps. It had to go somewhere he could find it again if he needed to. He counted twenty-five steps—fourteen plus eleven, Amy's age plus his own—and strayed off the path into the underbrush that framed the stairway. He found an indentation in the ground and nestled it there, covering it with stones and loose branches. Not the best hiding place, but it would have to do.

Dan got back on the steps just as a monk and three kung fu students came into view. They passed him at a run without a second look.

He speeded his descent. The way down was sweat free — and much, much faster. He would have been able to make even better time, except that he kept pausing to marvel at the miniature in his waistband. His mother's face, yet not his mother.

Amy had to see it. Whatever their disagreements over the contest, she wouldn't be able to ignore this. It was a lightning strike.

No sooner had he set foot on the telescope platform at the bottom than he spotted Jonah jogging toward him. His father followed several yards behind, hampered by the effort of running and texting at the same time.

"Where were you, cuz?" Jonah called urgently. "What were you doing up there?"

"Well —" Dan hesitated, not sure what he dare reveal.

Luckily, the star was in too much of a rush to wait for an answer. "Find your clothes and lose those pajamas. We're out."

"Where are we going?" Dan asked.

"I'll let you know the deal on the plane. We've got a date — with an army."

CHAPTER 15

The Great Wall.

Even seeing it from the bus, Amy had been unable to appreciate its vastness. It had been built as protection from the Mongols, its ribbon cutting clear across ancient China's vast northern frontier.

Now, walking along the ramparts of the Badaling section, Amy could see why even the Mongol hordes had thought twice before trying to attack this place. For starters, the Wall was thick—the top was as wide as the living room of their apartment back in Boston. That meant the Chinese could pack it with soldiers. There were towers every half mile or so. These served as observation posts, barracks, armories, and storehouses for supplies. The defenders could live on the Wall indefinitely.

It was also high—at least thirty feet at Badaling. Any attacking army would have to climb that distance through a barrage of arrows and boiling oil.

Dan should see this, she reflected. Arrows and boiling oil were just his speed. Yet it wasn't only the Wall's military history that made her think of her brother. Rarely did a full minute pass without her recalling their ugly fight in Tiananmen Square.

And now Dan was gone. Well, not exactly. He hadn't vanished into thin air. She knew who he was with, if not where he was.

An unpleasant memory returned — the murky picture of a slimy ridged body and long reptilian tail. An eighteen-foot Nile crocodile, viewed by moonlight.

Jonah Wizard could not be trusted. No Cahill could.

It had been more than two days since she'd last seen her brother. Their longest separation since the day Mom brought the little dweeb home from the hospital to ruin her life. Now it was starting to sink in that, without Dan, she had no life.

She thought back to their grandmother's funeral, the day when she and Dan had first learned about the search for the 39 Clues. They may have signed on as a sort of tribute to Grace, but, by the time the hunt had taken them to Paris, both believed with all their hearts that the contest was the most important thing on the face of the earth.

With each passing hour, Amy was becoming increasingly convinced that the whole business meant less than nothing if she couldn't get her brother back.

Where are you, Dan? Is this my fault? Are you so mad that you're never coming back?

She recalled his exact words: *I hate you!* It didn't get much clearer than that.

She couldn't blame him for hating her for what she'd said about Mom and Dad. In a weird way, she was almost proud of him for defending them when she couldn't.

To be relieved their parents were dead. The mere fact that she could think such a thing was like a business card with MADRIGAL printed on it.

"I can't put you down, Saladin, so stop asking," Nellie was muttering irritably. "It's too crowded. You'll get lost."

"Mrrp," Saladin complained.

Crowded. Amy shuddered. Was it ever! Their bus had turned out to be one of hundreds. Near the main parking area, tourists had swarmed like a plague of locusts among guides, souvenir vendors, and security guards. And the *stuff!* The Wall itself might have been an unspoiled ancient wonder, but beside it the goods for sale would have filled fifty malls — paper cuttings ranging from postcard size to large murals; intricate carvings from walnut shells; pictures made of seashells and feathers; silk kites, toys, figurines; traditional Chinese puzzle boxes by the thousands. Some of it was beautiful folk art; some of it was cheap junk. All of it had throngs of customers lined up with credit cards and fistfuls of yuan. The crush made Tiananmen Square seem empty by comparison. Amy had very nearly lost it. Only the refrain in her head had kept her focused: *Jonah draws a crowd . . . find Jonah and you've found Dan. . . .*

But so far, the crowds had been sightseers, not Wizard fans. Around here, the Great Wall outdrew teenage moguls, even the wonderful and celebrated Wiz.

Nellie peered over the parapet at the purple-tinged mountain vista that seemed to go on forever. "Pretty slick. From here you could spot an invading army twenty miles away. Are you sure those emperors were Janus? This place has Lucian written all over it."

Amy shook her head. "Way back then there was no Lucian *or* Janus. The Wall was started two thousand years before Gideon Cahill was even born."

The au pair shot her a cockeyed smile. "I forgot that there are still a few things on this planet you Cahills haven't had a hand in." The sun was low in the sky now, and she had to squint to see the next tower. "Looks like a big mob ahead. Maybe it's God's gift to hip-hop."

Amy nodded but said nothing. To her, the setting sun meant only one thing: They had been wandering around the Wall all afternoon, with no sign of Jonah — or Dan.

They raced along the ancient battlement — this stretch arduously uphill. Nellie set Saladin down, and the cat, happy to stretch his legs, bounded beside them. Puffing hard, they caught up to the horde assembled outside the tower — a Brazilian tour group.

"Jo-Jo—?" This time Amy's stammer had as much to do with breathlessness as the presence of a large group of people.

"Jonah Wizard," Nellie finished, scooping Saladin

back into her arms. "Have you seen him?"

"The Wiz?" The tour guide brightened. "He is here? I read his *O Filho Da Gangsta* bedtime stories to my nieces in São Paolo."

Nellie was totally disgusted. "No matter where you go, or who you meet, it's all Jonah, all the time."

"But," Amy added, barely able to lift her gaze from the cobblestones, "when you really need him, he's nowhere."

The au pair recognized the hopelessness in the girl's voice. "Okay," she said, taking charge. "We're tired. It's time to admit that we're not going to find Dan today. We have to figure out where we're going to sleep so we'll be fresh to take up the search in the morning."

Amy stuck out her jaw. "No! I'm not leaving here without my brother!"

"Be sensible. It'll be dark soon. We won't improve our chances of getting to Dan if we kill ourselves. We need rest and we need food. We haven't eaten since breakfast. You know how cranky Saladin gets when he's hungry."

Saladin added a plaintive "*mrrp!*" to the conversation.

"That cat eats too much already!" Amy erupted. "Fresh snapper, shrimp dumplings — what's next, beluga caviar? We don't have time for breaks! Who knows what Jonah could be doing to Dan right now? If he harms my brother in any way, I swear I'll put my hands around his throat and strangle him!"

Her breath caught in shock at the violence of her tone, and — worse — the realization that she meant every word. Was the Madrigal in her coming to the surface? Ordinary people tossed words like *strangle* around casually, not meaning anything by them. It was different for Madrigals. Madrigals *killed*.

"So with all that we have to worry about," she mumbled in a quieter tone, "you'll have to forgive me for not dropping everything because *Saladin's* a little hungry. He could live for a month on his own blubber. The last thing he needs is another snack."

A few feet away, a tourist unwrapped a sardine sandwich. With a *"mrrp!"* that was practically the shriek of a hunting bobcat, the Egyptian Mau hurled himself out of Nellie's grasp. Unaccustomed to hunting for his food, Saladin overshot the sandwich, skimmed the parapet at the edge of the Wall, and disappeared over the side.

Twin screams escaped Amy and Nellie.

They raced to the edge and looked down, terrified of what they might see.

Thirty feet below, Grace Cahill's beloved pet stood on the spot where invading armies had been repelled and slaughtered. His tail was high in the air; his fur bristled in outrage. The *"mrrp!"* he emitted was the most thorough scolding either of them had ever received.

"You know," Amy said, her voice shaking, "maybe we should get something to eat and find a hotel for the night."

CHAPTER 16

The city of Xian was much smaller than Beijing, but Dan could hardly tell the difference out the window of the G5. There was no towering skyline like the one in China's capital, but the sprawl of buildings seemed infinite, the red of brake lights clogging every inch of the grid of roadways. Traffic.

Pollution, too, he thought as the plane descended through a thick layer of brownish haze.

"Oh, no—" They weren't even on the runway, and Jonah's father was already immersed in his BlackBerry. "Remember those 'Live Large with the Wiz Generation' posters? Well, guess how that translates into Chinese—'Jonah Wizard Makes Your Ancestors Fat.'"

Dan brayed a laugh in his face. "Can you save me one? It'll go great in my collection!"

Broderick was not amused. "In that case, why don't *you* take the conference call from the record company?"

"It's all good, Pops." Jonah yawned as the jet touched down. "You know the drill. I take some lucky fan out to dinner; we post the whole thing on YouTube; everybody forgets about a few posters."

"They printed over six hundred thousand," his father reminded him, tight-lipped.

"Dinner and a movie," Jonah amended. "Better yet, clubbing in Xian. We'll give MTV Asia an exclusive. It'll be epic, yo! Just as soon as we're done with these terracotta homeys," he added with a wink at Dan.

Of all the managers, publicists, and bodyguards of the Wizard entourage, and even Jonah's own father, the star had chosen Dan to accompany him on this mission to learn the secret of the terracotta army.

Not that Dan cared about the Clue hunt anymore.

Another thing about Xian — they had real limos here. A silver stretch was waiting at the airport to take them to their hotel, the Bell Tower, where Jonah had reserved the entire top floor.

Jonah's father was on the phone with the hotel's nightclub to hire the headline act to perform for them in their suite — a little dinner entertainment.

Dan glanced at his watch. Seven-thirty. "How late does this terracotta place stay open?"

Jonah flashed his rock star grin. "It closed two hours ago. We can't go yet. It isn't dark enough."

Dan's voice dropped. "I get it. We have to check it out when there's no one around."

"That's how I know we're family," Jonah approved. "Cahills think alike, yo. Got a good feeling about us working together. We make a fly team."

If this were Amy, Dan reflected mournfully, she'd be telling him how stupid he was, calling him dweeb while she went to some library to check out six hundred books on terracotta warriors.

His mood darkened abruptly. Then she'd accuse their poor parents of deserving their fate. How could she even *think* that about Mom and Dad? He patted his pocket where the picture from Bodhidharma's cave lay hidden. "You know, Jonah," he ventured, "it's been—uh—two days, four hours, twenty-one minutes—"

"Since you last saw your sis," Jonah finished sympathetically.

"Not that I'm keeping track," Dan added quickly.

"Must be hard," the star agreed. "I've got to tell you, cuz, I'm amazed we haven't come up with her yet. By now—it's almost like she doesn't want to be found."

Dan recoiled as if he had just been slapped.

His distress was interrupted by a knock at the door. The entertainment had arrived.

Dan had little appetite at first. He sat at the table, viciously dismantling dumplings with his chopsticks, eating next to nothing as he mulled over the devastating notion that Amy might have written him off. Was that possible? She called him annoying often enough. Yet he said the same about her, and he would have given anything to be reunited with his sister.

The show turned out to be Chinese acrobats who executed an unbelievable climbing-and-tumbling routine. It was off the chain—Jonah's words. Even Dan began to climb out of his funk, especially for the grand finale—a dragon dance performed upside down while hanging from the ceiling.

Jonah's father invited a few local entertainment reporters to join the fun, so Jonah was sure to get good press in Xian—as if Jonah got bad press anywhere.

The man of the hour was at his schmoozing best, laughing and joking with the media. No way could anybody tell that, as soon as this was over, he was off to burglarize the most important archaeological site in Asia. Yet when no one was looking, Dan couldn't help but notice a glazed expression on the famous face.

Funny—I think the rock star lifestyle is amazing, but it has to be brutal twenty-four/seven. For Jonah, this was the normal routine. It was probably exhausting to be at fever pitch, day after day, week after week.

It was past midnight by the time the acrobats had gone home and the reporters had finished their interviews. Dan was rummaging through the minibar when the sound of distant music reached him. Not Jonah's music—in fact, the melody was classical. To Dan's astonishment, he recognized the piece. It was by Mozart, perhaps the greatest of Jonah's Janus relatives.

He followed the sound to the suite's smallest bedroom and peered inside. Broderick Wizard perched on the edge of the bed, an acoustic guitar in his arms, his fingers a blur over the nylon strings. It was obvious—even to Dan, who knew nothing about music—that Jonah's father was playing with great skill.

"You're awesome."

Broderick looked up in surprise. "Oh—it's you." He set the guitar down on the comforter, picked up his BlackBerry, and began self-consciously scrolling through e-mail.

"Does Jonah know how good you are?" Dan asked.

Jonah's father cleared his throat uncomfortably and tried to hide behind the pocket-size device. "I was quite the rising star in college. But then I met Cora, and . . . well, I'm decent, but, you know, compared to *them*—"

Them. The Janus. Why play music if you can't be Mozart, or Scott Joplin, or John Lennon, or Jonah Wizard? What a Cahill attitude!

Dan was surprised to feel genuine sympathy for Jonah's father. Whatever dreams he might have had were gone, traded for a spot on the red carpet a half step behind his famous son. And what was left for Broderick? Thumb cramps, maybe, from texting.

It made Dan wonder about his own father. He remembered very little about either of his parents, but, like Broderick, Arthur Trent had been an outsider who married into the Cahill family. When people talked about Dad, he was always just Mom's partner, working with Grace in the Clue hunt. He'd even raised his kids with the legal name Cahill, just as Grace had done with her daughter. What else had he given up to play in the big leagues with the Cahill heavy hitters?

Jonah appeared in the doorway behind Dan. "You

guys having a secret meeting without me?" His eyes fell on the guitar lying on the bedspread.

His father looked uncomfortable. "I was just—you know—killing time."

"He's amazing!" Dan enthused. "Not all your talent comes from the Janus side, Jonah. You should hear your dad play. He's good enough to—"

"Great, cuz," Jonah interrupted firmly. "Let's bounce. The car's waiting for us outside."

His father nodded in resignation. "Let's go."

It was 12:25 A.M. when the silver stretch pulled away from the curb in front of the Bell Tower Hotel.

"Tell the driver to stop short of the terracotta museum," Jonah advised his father. "We can hoof it a couple of blocks. Last thing we need is cops nosing around our ride."

"Got it," Broderick confirmed. "Good luck, guys."

"Luck's got nothing to do with it," Jonah replied with supreme confidence.

They drove about twenty minutes before the driver called out that they were getting close.

Dan squinted through the window. "There's no museum coming up. Wait—you mean *that* thing?"

The structure that loomed out of the darkness was low and absolutely enormous—at least five blocks wide and stretching back as far as they could see.

"They built a giant airplane hangar over the whole dig," Jonah's father explained. "The biggest in the world."

"Crazy," Jonah commented. "Okay, we'll roll from here. Ready, cuz?"

"Let's do it," Dan replied.

They got out, keeping to the shadows. The limo backed away to a spot behind some bushes.

They made their way swiftly and silently toward the hangar. It was farther away than it looked — its sheer size created the illusion of closeness. Both were breathing hard as they mounted the front steps and concealed themselves behind the ticket booths.

Jonah reached into the pocket of his black leather jacket and pulled out a device that resembled a larger version of his father's BlackBerry.

"Is that to call your dad when we're done?" Dan asked.

"It's a heat sensor," Jonah explained in a low tone. "A place like this has got to be crawling with guards. We can keep track of them on this screen."

Dan peered at the readout. The vast complex was mostly in darkness, but there were at least seven or eight heat signatures inside and outside the building. Several of them seemed to be bunched together.

Dan was alarmed. "Do they see us?"

Jonah watched as tiny but very bright flickers appeared around the group. "I think they're on a tea break."

"Yeah, but where?" Dan persisted.

"In the back. Come on, cuz, we may never get a better chance!" Jonah produced two lumps of putty and affixed them to the lock on the glass doors, kneading them together. There was a sizzling sound, and he whipped his hand away. Smoke issued from the spot as the chemical reaction burned the lock away.

"I thought you guys were just into art," Dan said.

Jonah shrugged. "Depends what you call art, yo. Burglary can be an art. We jacked this stuff from the Ekats." He pushed the door open. They were inside.

Dan gawked. Laid out before them was a most astonishing sight. It was like looking at a vast crowd of people—in Fenway Park, maybe. But they weren't real. An entire army of soldiers, horses, and chariots, all made of off-white earthenware. Thousands of them, lined up in tight ranks and forever on guard.

Jonah dragged him into a crouch. "Cuz—we're not tourists!"

"This is the most amazing thing I've ever seen!" Dan breathed.

"I've seen better," Jonah told him, "by my own branch."

"Yeah, but there are so many of them!"

"Yo, here's the plan: You check out the warrior in row thirty-eight, space fifty-three of the first pit."

Dan looked worried. "What about you?"

"I've got you," Jonah promised. "I'll be right behind, monitoring the guards. Hurry!"

That made sense to Dan. He scrambled under the railing and dropped down into the huge excavation pit, where the warriors towered over him, each one unique.

He flashed a sign at Jonah and began to count rows, hiding himself among the tall figures. The detail was astounding. The facial features, hairstyles, and clothing textures were all distinctive. He passed a kneeling archer and was amazed to note that there was a tread pattern on the bottom of the figure's shoe. From close up, he could see that the warriors had been painted, although the colors had faded over the centuries. Jonah's father had told them that the terracotta army was more than two thousand years old. According to legend, each statue had been built around a living soldier. It was very cool, in an ultra-creepy way—burying thousands of warriors with their emperor to protect him in the afterlife. As Dan threaded his way between the figures, he imagined a skeleton at the heart of each one—a real army of the dead.

Concentrate! If you lose count, you'll have to go back to start! Thirty-one . . . thirty-two . . . thirty-three . . .

He peered over his shoulder, but Jonah was out of sight. How much longer could the guards' break go on? Jonah's heat sensor wouldn't be of much help if they were spotted.

Row 38. He made a right turn and began to count his way across the ranks. *One . . . two . . . three . . .*

The almond-shaped eyes were blank and unmoving as he passed by. Yet he couldn't escape the feeling that he was being watched.

CHAPTER 17

Jonah lay flat on his stomach, keeping one eye on the heat sensor and the other on Dan. The kid had guts—you had to give him props for that, even if he was too dumb to know he was being used.

No, he corrected himself. *Poor little orphan. Bad luck, that's all.* It wasn't as if Dan and his sister ever had a shot at being big players in the scheme of things. Jonah had earned his success, sure. But it hadn't hurt to be the son of Cora Wizard, the Janus leader. He'd been born with his foot in every door in the arts.

Find the thirty-nine clues, and you won't need anybody's connections. You'll be your own man.

More like your own Superman.

The hangar was in night mode, with most of the lights out. Anybody else scanning the ranks of soldiers would probably miss seeing short, scrawny Dan Cahill in between the larger terracotta figures.

Pretty wild to build a fake army to protect a dead guy. But as a Janus, Jonah had to respect the ancient Chinese who had set this up. *Very* sweet. From his vantage point over the pits, the endless rows of soldiers looked almost like one of his concert audiences — except, of course, they weren't going totally apewire.

He checked the monitor. The tea break was still in progress, but that couldn't last much longer.

Hurry up, cuz . . .

He squinted at the sensor. Pretty tight technology, but there were still some bugs to iron out. You could see everybody, yet it was hard to judge the perspective. He was pretty sure the guards were out back. But on the monitor, they appeared dead center and higher up. Two other security people on the side pathways, also toward the rear. The smaller, moving blip was Dan. But —

He frowned. Who was that bright spot over there? If this guy was at the back, shouldn't his heat signature appear near the top, by the tea drinkers?

Jonah tapped the sensor in annoyance. This dumb gizmo made it seem like there was an extra person right smack-dab in the middle of the terracotta army!

And the Dan Cahill blip was heading directly toward him. . . .

Twenty-seven . . . twenty-eight . . . twenty-nine . . .

Dan pushed through the ranks of warriors, nearly tripping over the hoof of a terracotta horse. When he righted himself, he ended up scraping his chin against the elbow of the archer in the row in front of him.

According to Jonah's father, all these warriors had originally been armed with real weapons. *I could have just sliced my head off!* Certainly, it would have been even harder to move through these tight ranks if they were filled with razor-sharp swords and spear points.

Dan scrambled over an unexcavated mound. *Forty-seven . . . forty-eight . . . just a few more, now . . .* He peered ahead in an attempt to pick out number fifty-three.

He saw the battle mace first—a heavy spiked iron ball attached by a chain to a wooden handle.

Maybe a few of them are still armed. . . .

This thought was quickly replaced by another: *If this is number fifty-three, maybe the weapon is the clue!*

Eagerly, he scrambled toward it. Just as he noticed that this figure was shorter than the others, terracotta warrior number fifty-three *moved.*

The astonishment paralyzed Dan for an instant. And by the time he came out of it, the mace was hurtling through the air on a collision course with his head. With a gasp, Dan ducked, and the lethal spikes went singing past his ear. A warrior's elbow shattered. The hand and forearm fell to the ground.

No bones, no dead guy inside, Dan thought—when he should have been concentrating on survival.

The imposter hefted his weapon for another strike. Through his terror, Dan could see that his assailant was clad in head-to-toe padded foam, colored to match the fading paint of the terracotta army. He wore a full mask made of rubber, designed to mimic the faces and expressions of the statues. From close range, it was not a great likeness. But standing amid thousands of his fellow soldiers, it would have been impossible to pick him out.

"Who are you?" Dan rasped.

His answer was another attack from the mace, a devastating swipe that missed only by inches. Dan felt a stab of pain as the chain burned along his arm.

All rational thought disappeared from Dan's mind, save for one:

Run.

A trap! Jonah's eyes were riveted to the small screen where the heat signatures of Dan and his assailant played out the chase. The security people hadn't noticed them yet, but how long would that last?

I've got to get out of here!

He was on his feet in a heartbeat, sprinting for the front door where he had burned away the lock. And from there, the turnstiles, the limo, the hotel — it was all going to be okay. . . .

He froze in his tracks. Dan. How could he leave him in danger?

Forget Dan! You brought him in case it was a trap!

Dan was an eleven-year-old kid. He was only down in that pit because Jonah had sent him there.

Boo-hoo, life's rough. You're a big player! Cora Wizard's son! The only chance for the Janus in the clue hunt —

He threw open the door. The cool air of the outside beckoned. Freedom; safety . . .

Awww!

Jonah spun around and ran back inside, jumping down into the pit. Through the rows of warriors he dashed, using the heat sensor to guide him.

His mind whirled. *If I get killed in China, the press is going to have a field day!* Mingled with a more urgent thought: *Hang on, cuz! I'm coming!*

When he came upon the attacker, he almost rear-ended him. Whoa, the guy was dressed up like one of the statues! Jonah's eyes bulged. The fake warrior was twirling a mace, ready to smash Dan's head in.

"Yo!" he called.

The imposter spun around, and the mace shattered the face of the terracotta swordsman beside him.

Dan jumped up and threw himself onto the imposter's back. Enraged, the man jabbed at him with the wooden handle.

Jonah grabbed two fistfuls of the foam costume and pulled with all his strength. The material tore away, revealing track pants and a sweatshirt. The man swung at him with his free hand, landing a dizzying blow on Jonah's cheek. The star went down, landing in a terracotta chariot, stunned.

With a violent twist, the imposter threw Dan off his back and wheeled menacingly. Dan tried to scramble up again but whacked his forehead on the clay hoof of a battle horse. The attacker raised his mace high over his head, ready to bring it down with crushing force.

Dan knew a moment of perfect horror. He was going to die. He was too hemmed in to roll away, and the imposter's momentum was unstoppable.

Momentum. The abbot's voice echoed in Dan's mind. *The momentum of your adversary is your greatest ally.*

As the fake warrior loomed over him, arm high to deliver the fatal blow, Dan's foot shot up and lodged in his attacker's midsection. Dan's hands were next, grabbing the ripped foam of the costume so he could guide his assailant up and over him.

Dan was amazed at how little of his own force was required. Just as the wushu master had promised, the smaller Dan was able to launch his fully grown attacker fifteen feet down the row, wiping out warriors like tenpins. The man lay in the rubble, unconscious.

Dan and Jonah were on him in an instant. Jonah pried the mace handle from the foam glove. "That was some serious Jackie Chan, cuz!" the hip-hop star wheezed in awe.

"Let's get out of here!" Dan hissed.

"Not yet," said Jonah grimly. He yanked their prisoner's mask off and slapped him awake.

The man shrugged blankly. "No speak."

Dan reached into the man's fanny pack and pulled out a thick wad of hundred-euro notes. "Where did you get this?"

Jonah brandished the spiked ball of the mace. "We could jog your memory."

"Children!" the imposter babbled. "Boy and girl!"

"Got a name?" Jonah persisted.

"No name! Talk like Simon on *American Idol*!"

"British accent!" Dan breathed. "The Kabras—they set you up, Jonah!"

"They set us both up," the star amended. "And now they're way ahead while we're in the wrong city, fighting for our lives."

"We'll pay them back," Dan promised. "But first we've got to get out of this—"

His sentence was interrupted by the loudest alarm either of them had ever heard. At the first sound of the Klaxon, their captive was up and gone, hopping along the rows, ripping off his costume as he ran.

Jonah and Dan needed no further encouragement. They were off at a sprint, heading for the front exit.

Security guards swarmed the pathways. Flashlight beams crisscrossed the pits. The emergency lighting came on. There was no place to hide.

Jonah tripped over one of the figures and went down. Dan hauled him up. The two cousins clambered out of the pit onto a strip of unexcavated ground. It was a footrace now as they made it to the entrance and blasted through the unlocked door.

Jonah leaped the turnstile—right into the arms of a policeman. A second officer scooped up Dan.

They were caught.

CHAPTER 18

The holding cell was tiny and smelled bad. This may or may not have been because the toilet was right in the middle of the room, displayed like it was a stylish conversation piece. Dan hoped he wouldn't be there long enough to have to use it.

If Dan was upset, Jonah was devastated. His fans would not have recognized their hip-hop idol, who sat on the wooden bench, his famous face sinking lower with each passing hour. Gone was his effervescent confidence. In fact, he wasn't speaking at all. To Dan, who had only known Jonah the world-beater, the change was almost as scary as their current predicament.

Dan tried to be encouraging. "Your dad was parked just down the block. He must have seen what happened. I'll bet he's on his BlackBerry right now, pulling strings to get us out of jail."

"Yeah, whatever," Jonah mumbled.

Dan was bewildered. "Don't you want to get out of here?"

Jonah shrugged. "I don't care."

"Well, you ought to care! You've got the world's greatest life to get back to! You're a rap star, a TV star—"

"You think that means anything?" Jonah interrupted. "Seriously, yo, in our family, if you can't hack it with the thirty-nine clues, you're nothing!"

"Fine," Dan conceded. "Ian and Natalie put one over on us. So what?"

Jonah was bitter. "So what if I stink at the thing I've been prepping for since the day I was born? Yeah, put me in a recording studio — double platinum. Put me on TV — hit show. Put me in the clue hunt—"

"Who cares about the clue hunt?" Dan interrupted. "After all you've accomplished, you're a failure because you don't think you're acing the clue hunt?"

"I *am* a failure!" Jonah stormed. "As a Cahill *and* a person! Don't you get it? I bailed on you tonight!"

"You didn't! You probably saved my life!"

"I was halfway out the door, cuz," Jonah insisted. "Okay, I came back. But I was gone."

"That *proves* you're not bad," Dan reasoned. "Any idiot can do the right thing. You know what's hard? Doing the right thing when you've been hardwired to do the wrong one!" Who better than a Madrigal to understand that?

"I flaked on an eleven-year-old kid who I set up to get killed!"

Dan took a step back. "You wanted me *dead*?"

The famous features twisted. "You were supposed to be my decoy. If the guards spot us, I throw you to the sharks and bounce. Nothing personal," he added, noting Dan's hurt expression. "It's the clues, yo. They're supposed to make you the most powerful human in history — I say they make you *less* than human!"

Dan said nothing, mostly because there was nothing he *could* say. He wasn't even all that angry at Jonah. Dan knew better than anybody how the Clue hunt could mess with your head. Look how it had turned Amy against their parents and split up two siblings who had scarcely left each other's company for eleven years. Dan couldn't escape a growing dread that this wasn't a temporary separation — that there was a very real chance that he might never see his sister again.

At the same time, he had saved his own life in hand-to-hand combat, using skills taught to him by a Shaolin master — how awesome was that?

There was a clatter of metal on metal, and the guard appeared, accompanied by Broderick Wizard.

"Are you guys okay?"

His famous son didn't even look up, but to Dan, the man was a welcome sight. This was the closest Dan would ever come to having a dad show up in the nick of time.

"We're all right," Dan told Broderick. "Thanks for getting us out."

Jonah's father marched them briskly through the building toward the waiting limo. Their quick pace and the dirty looks they were receiving from all the police officers plainly said that they were making their getaway before the cops changed their minds.

"Don't even ask what the record company had to say about this," Broderick informed his son as the limo pulled away from the station. "They called in favors they'll still be repaying twenty years down the road."

Jonah slumped against the leather upholstery. "I thought the 'gangsta' image was good for sales."

"Not in China," Broderick growled. "They take their terracotta warriors very seriously. And you turned six of them into dust."

"Blame the Kabras," Dan said defensively. "And the hit man they hired."

"Well, he must have escaped," Jonah's father concluded, "because this whole rap is on your heads. And you wouldn't believe what it cost to make it go away. Venice hit the ceiling! The Janus haven't had a cover-up this big since Lufbery's lion got loose in Piccadilly!"

Jonah's answer was a soft purring snore. He hadn't slept a wink all night. Neither had Dan, but never could he remember being so wired—not even the time he'd put away forty ounces of Red Bull. He watched the sun rise over the miles of apartment buildings in Xian on both sides of the walls of the old city. The dawn of a new day that he had almost not lived to see. It felt— *big*.

Jonah woke up as the limo stopped in front of the Bell Tower. He followed along like a zombie as they took the private elevator up to the penthouse.

"There's a surprise waiting for you in the room," Broderick promised his son.

"And I've got a surprise for *you*. I'm out. No more clue hunt for this kid. I don't want it and I don't like what it's turning me into. Tell Mom she's going to have to find another chump."

At that moment, the elevator door slid aside, leading them directly into the suite, and a strong female voice declared, "Why don't you tell me yourself, Jonah?"

Jonah's eyes widened. *"Mom?"*

Cora Wizard, internationally renowned sculptor and performance artist. The youngest Nobel laureate in history. Legendary leader of the Janus branch.

The woman standing before them looked a lot like — Dan did a double take — a hippie?

Yeah! Her shoulder-length hair was pulled back with a headband. She wore a simple, loose-fitting tunic. *This* was Jonah's mother?

But on closer inspection, her ordinary appearance concealed the bearing of a five-star general. Her black eyes moved like the targeting mechanism of a laser-guided missile launcher. Around her neck hung a rope dangling a copper modern art piece — one of the many she was famous for. And, at her instant command, an army of the world's most brilliant and creative people — thousands of actors, musicians, directors, writers, painters, comedians, sculptors, magicians, and swash-buckling showmen of all stripes.

"You have to find someone else to win the contest for the Janus," Jonah said plaintively. "I can't do it anymore."

"It's good to see you, too, son who's been away for three months," Cora replied sarcastically. She turned her penetrating gaze on Dan. "And I can't tell you how happy I am finally to meet Grace's grandson."

"You're not listening, Mom," Jonah interjected.

"I'm multitasking, dear." She cut him off in a voice that was at once motherly and tempered steel. "You'll have the help you need soon enough." To Dan, she went on, "You and your sister are the pride of the family. Everybody's raving about how you're holding your own in the clue hunt. And at last we understand why."

Dan waited. What was she talking about?

"For all these weeks, you've been wondering which Cahill branch you belong to. Well, the mystery is over. Our genealogy department has proven once and for all that you and your sister are Janus. Welcome to our clan!"

Her husband applauded, and even Jonah smiled. "That's tight, cuz. I knew you had it going on."

Dan nodded weakly. Janus? But that was impossible! He knew his branch all too well. He would have given anything to change that awful truth, but wishing didn't make it so.

Why was Cora Wizard lying to him? Not that the deception bothered him. He expected that from any Cahill. But why *this* lie? Was she trying to recruit the Cahill kids to jumpstart the Janus effort for the 39 Clues? This was a woman with wushu masters at her beck and call, fencers and expert marksmen. She could pick up the phone and have Steven Spielberg, Justin Timberlake, and half of Hollywood on a plane to China. What did she need Amy and Dan for? Were they really that good? Half the time, it felt like they were in way over their heads, bickering about nonsense because their true situation was just too awful. Parents dead; grandmother dead; fugitives from Massachusetts Social Services; and now their only asset — their strength as a unit — taken from them.

"Well?" Cora prodded. "Don't you have anything to say?"

He stared at her, mesmerized, the doomed fly in the spider's thrall. He looked away from the burning black eyes and found himself gazing at the copper piece on the end of her necklace.

Weird — it seemed familiar somehow. But that didn't make sense. This was the first time he'd ever laid eyes on Jonah's mother.

When the distant memory came back, it struck him like a hammer blow, and he actually staggered from the impact. He'd been only four, but he would never forget. The metal sculpture, one of the handful of objects that survived the fire. The artwork with the bug — the listening device.

Cora's necklace is a miniature replica of that sculpture!

The sculpture had come from Cora, her personal design! A gift, she had probably called it. And all the time it had been a ruse to spy on his parents — part of an escalating cycle of surveillance and coercion that ended with the fire that devoured Hope and Arthur and left their children orphans.

No, Cora hadn't set that fire. But only because Isabel Kabra had beaten her to it. They were *all* guilty — all those Cahills who let their blind ambition and craving for power fuel the runaway train that was the search for the 39 Clues. It was that unstoppable juggernaut — as much as any flaming match — that had killed Mom and Dad.

When at last he found his voice, it was the voice of a much taller, much older young man, as if he had aged ten years in the past ten seconds. He had been blind before, but it was crystal clear to him now. Jonah's father had *never* tried to find Amy. They had been keeping him, using him like a puppet on a string. And now along came this horrible woman who had participated in the confrontation that had led to the death of his parents. And she had the *nerve* to welcome him to her poisonous family.

"Janus?" he spat contemptuously. "I'm no Janus! I know *exactly* what branch I am!" He stormed to the open elevator and turned for a parting shot. He was so full of emotion that it was out before he could stop himself:

"I'm a Madrigal!"

The last thing he saw before the doors swept shut was the first family of the Janus frozen in openmouthed shock.

CHAPTER 19

The fine for dropping a cat off the Great Wall of China turned out to be four hundred yuan—about fifty-nine US dollars. Amy and Nellie also paid a hundred-yuan tip to the soldier who went down to bring Saladin back to them, plus another forty-three and change to buy ointment and bandages for the scratches he received.

Their hotel was really more of a guest cottage—just barely adequate. It was called the Golden Monkey. It didn't have monkeys, but a couple of the cockroaches could have passed for pygmy marmosets.

Amy barely noticed the dingy, cramped room and the bugs. The only thing on her mind was Dan.

"We blew it, Nellie," she exclaimed, staring out the fly-specked window at the distant ramparts of the Great Wall. "We took a gamble and we lost. For some reason, Jonah blew off that trip to the Wall. Or we were in a different part. And by now he could be anywhere. They might not even be in China anymore. For all we know, we're on the wrong continent."

Nellie was at the tiny desk, hunched over Dan's

laptop computer. "Hey, come and look at this."

"You found Jonah?" Amy asked eagerly.

"No. But I've been thinking about your idea—that Puyi was working on something Cahill when he got turfed out of the Forbidden City. And that we might be able to take a guess at it by looking at major world events around 1924."

"I don't care," Amy groaned. "I just want Dan back."

Nellie looked up sharply. "Hey, little girl, you get a grip. The clue hunt isn't over, and it's doubly important now. Remember, Jonah's still on it, which makes it the best way to pick up Dan's trail. Now, I've made a list of some of the top news headlines from the early 1920s. See if any of this rings a bell in the Cahill world."

Chastened, Amy got up to join her. Of course her au pair was right. Without a lead pointing directly to Dan, all they could do was pursue the 39 Clues in the hope that Dan would do the same.

She peered down at the screen:

20-ton meteorite lands near Blackstone, Virginia.
Egypt gains independence.
President Harding dies in office.
Construction begins on Yankee Stadium.
George Mallory and Andrew Irvine lost on
   Mount Everest.
Great Kanto earthquake devastates Japan.
First US execution using poison gas.
J. Edgar Hoover appointed head of FBI.

Amy read the full three-page list and sat back with a sigh. "I don't know. I think Grace may have mentioned some of these things over the years, but I can't be sure. The truth is, she's only been dead a couple of months, and already I'm having trouble remembering the sound of her voice."

Saladin rubbed up against her leg and emitted a sympathetic "*mrrp.*"

"So what should we do?" she asked worriedly.

Nellie shrugged. "We'll go back to the Wall. We're already here. We might as well give it one more try."

Amy nodded. They had no other leads—for Dan *or* the Clue hunt. If they came up empty today, they would be completely adrift.

○————◯◯————○

The pounding punk rock chords were tinny and distorted through the tiny speaker.

"Hi, this is Nellie. I'm probably off tasting food you've never heard of, or listening to music that would blow your mind. So what are you waiting for? Leave a message."

The beep cut right to Dan's heart. He slumped against the glass of the pay phone booth, hoping against hope that the cell phone problem had been fixed—that the message was a mistake, and the au pair's familiar voice would cut in.

"It's me—Dan," he stammered. "Sorry I haven't called sooner. I thought Jonah's dad was leaving messages for me. It's a long story. I'm in—well, I guess that doesn't matter because I have to find you guys now. Uh . . . see you later — I hope."

He hung up and immediately wrenched the receiver from its cradle and added, "I miss you!" But it was too late. The connection was already broken.

The streets of downtown Xian had been deserted when Dan had stormed out of the Bell Tower Hotel. They were crowded now, like Boston at the height of rush hour. Peddlers clogged the sidewalks; bizarre food smells issued from every storefront; plucked chickens hung next to state-of-the-art cell phones in display windows. The sounds were loud and discordant. Bicycles and motor scooters battled buses for road space.

Being alone, a foreign kid amid all this chaos, should have been frightening to Dan. Instead, all he felt was anger, most of it directed at himself.

What have I done?

He had trusted Jonah, who had always proved to be untrustworthy. And he had run away from Amy when he should have stuck by her. Standing alone on this street, it seemed like the ultimate no-brainer — she was all he had in the world, and he was the same for her.

Now it was too late. He had no way of finding Amy, no way to know what leads they were following, no way even to surrender to Social Services — or worse, Aunt Beatrice. Possibly the most dangerous of all, he had spilled the beans about their deepest, darkest secret. Now the word was out that he and Amy were Madrigals. And for what? The pleasure of seeing the

Wizards look shocked for two or three seconds?

He grinned in spite of himself. *It was a pretty great two or three seconds.*

But stupid. He was a target now. Amy, too.

I should have warned her.

Of course, who knew if Nellie was even checking her cell phone if it didn't work in China?

The cloudburst was sudden—sheets of rain pelting the Xian streets. Peddlers scrambled to protect their wares; pedestrians ran for cover. Dan wound up at the bottom of a half flight of stairs in a grungy basement-level video arcade. Okay—maybe this was just what he needed. Blasting a few spaceships might settle his nerves. And a little breakfast wouldn't hurt. His Chinese money would go at least that far.

As he examined the selection of candy bars on the rack by the cash register, his eyes focused on a large TV monitor tuned to CNN International.

What he saw very nearly stopped his heart.

This time Saladin did not complain about being carried around the Great Wall. The safety of Nellie's arms seemed like a pretty good place to the Egyptian Mau.

The crowds were just as dense as yesterday. It put Amy on edge, but not nearly as much as the fact that there was no Jonah and no indication that he would ever be coming. Somehow, the star's schedule must have changed. He was off in a different direction, dragging

Dan with him. Or, even scarier, abandoning Dan, leaving him on his own in this strange country. Not for the first time, she thought of the US Embassy in Beijing. Yes, it would mean a one-way trip to Social Services in Massachusetts. Yet if she was unable to scour the most populous nation in the world for a single lost eleven-year-old, she had to appeal to somebody who could.

The question was when. When was it time to turn this over to the professionals, people with the power to stage a major manhunt? It had been four full days since she'd last laid eyes on Dan.

They walked for miles, never stopping, always searching. The crowds thinned as they moved farther from the main tourist area of the Badaling section.

Amy's feet felt like blocks of granite and her spirits were even heavier. Giving up was unthinkable, but the Wall went on for thousands of miles.

A passing couple asked her to take their picture.

"Sure." She peered through the viewfinder of their expensive-looking camera and began to adjust the long telephoto lens. As she centered the frame around the posing subjects, the tower behind them came into sharp focus. She frowned at the Chinese character painted on the wooden door.

Why is that so familiar? I can't read Chinese.

As she snapped a couple of pictures and handed back the camera, it came to her.

"Nellie, isn't that the symbol that Alistair was doodling on his place mat yesterday?"

Nellie squinted at it. "I think you're right. But why would anybody write *charm* on an old door in the middle of the Great Wall?"

The lady tourist spoke up. "Charm? That's not the best translation. A better word might be—*grace.*"

At first glance this tower seemed no different from the dozens of others they had passed through—the stone husk of what had once been a guard station on the Mongolian frontier. The windows were small openings designed more for archers than for light. An ancient staircase led down into the base of the structure, which had probably once served as barracks and armory.

Nellie pointed. "Look." She indicated another flight of stairs heading to the top of the tower. That was unusual. They started up. At the landing, they came upon another door with the same *grace* symbol. Locked.

"Hold the cat." Nellie thrust Saladin into Amy's arms. From the pocket of her jeans, she pulled two bobby pins and began to work them into the skeleton-key lock. Amy was just reflecting that the au pair seemed awfully skilled at lock picking—and besides,

Nellie didn't wear bobby pins—when there was a click, and the door swung open.

They found themselves in a square room, windowless except for a round skylight directly overhead. There were six wooden tables of varying heights, and a clutter of clocks, crystal vases, tiny framed mirrors, figurines in glass boxes, and tall champagne flutes.

"Oh, God," groaned Nellie. "We've broken into somebody's garage sale."

Amy's brow furrowed. "It can't be a coincidence. Grace's name on the door and all this stuff up here. But what does it mean?"

"It's just a bunch of knickknacks—the kind of junk you find in an old lady's attic. I mean, you'd think that in the country that invented feng shui—"

"That's it!" Amy almost screamed. "Grace was totally into feng shui! She was constantly talking about how important it was to arrange your stuff to allow for positive energy flow."

"Her house always looked pretty good," Nellie admitted. "Until your nut-loaf relatives burned it down."

"It's way more than that!" Amy insisted, her excitement level rising. "Grace spent hours teaching me about feng shui. I think she knew that the clue hunt might bring me to this room one day."

Nellie was thunderstruck. "Are you saying that your grandmother put together a feng shui puzzle for you *ten thousand miles* from Massachusetts?"

Amy shook her head. "No, I think Grace found the

puzzle on her travels through China and marked the spot by painting her name on the doors."

"But if she didn't set this up, who did?"

Amy scoured the featureless walls, looking for some sort of hint as to who might have created this bizarre brainteaser. When she saw the faint letters scratched into the stone just about eye level, she laughed out loud. A name was spelled out in block capitals: HENRY.

Nellie was bewildered. "Who's Henry?"

"We just read about him, remember?" Amy explained breathlessly. "Henry is the English name Puyi adopted! This is the work of the last emperor himself! And the stuff looks modern, so he must have done all this near the end of his life, after he was released from prison!"

The au pair rolled her eyes. "Isn't that just like a Cahill? Why say something when you can turn it into a feng shui puzzle at the Great Wall of China?"

Amy handed Saladin back to her and pushed up her sleeves.

"Wait," said Nellie. "You're not going to try to rearrange this whole mess."

"Oh, yes I am. Grace made me an expert for a reason. There's only one problem. She had this special Chinese compass—a *luopan*, she called it. I don't have anything like that."

"How about that?" Nellie pointed straight down.

Tiled into the floor was an elaborate design of concentric circles, with hundreds of Chinese markings.

"That's it!" Amy breathed, eyes alight. "Grace's *luopan* had moving parts, so you could take it from house to house. This one's fixed, permanently aligned to magnetic north."

"I guess nobody's moving the Great Wall after two thousand years," Nellie conceded.

Amy set up the tables first, consulting the *luopan* constantly in order to get the corners in harmony with the Earth Plate and Heaven Dial. Then came the painstaking placement of the smaller pieces according to the feng shui principles of the flow of *qi*—energy.

She knew this wasn't a puzzle in the usual sense. There was no single solution. Many different arrangements would be correct and acceptable. But would all of them produce the result that Puyi had intended?

She was on to the figurines now, carefully turning them so that their faces were pointed in accordance with the twenty-four directions on the *luopan*'s dial.

At last, she stepped back and surveyed her handiwork.

"Now what?" asked Nellie.

Amy had no answer. Had she messed up the feng shui? Or was the whole idea wrong to begin with?

Nellie gave her a sympathetic smile. "Well, you may not win the clue hunt. But if I ever need an interior decorator, you've got the job."

Amy was bewildered. How could she have been mistaken about this? She'd been so sure.

She scrutinized the setup and leaned forward to

straighten a mirror that might have been tilted ever so slightly off the Red Cross Grid line. She stepped back and watched it happen.

A beam came straight down from the skylight, struck the mirror, and ricocheted around the array of objects. In an instant, the dim room was crisscrossed with brilliant rays.

"Whoa!" exclaimed Nellie.

Amy stared. The product of this symphony of refraction was an image projected on the gray wall at the *luopan*'s magnetic north. It was an inverted V, with one slope much steeper than the other.

"What is it?" Nellie asked.

To Amy, the silhouette was unmistakable.

"I know where the next clue is!" she breathed. From beneath her shirt, Amy drew out the folded silk message from the Forbidden City. Here, in the guts of the Great Wall, she had unlocked Puyi's explanation of the poem he had written as a much younger man.

"It's where the Earth meets the sky."

CHAPTER 20

The screen at the video arcade showed a tilted land-scape of pure white. A howling blizzard was in progress, roaring in the parka-clad CNN reporter's microphone so that he had to shout to be understood.

"The fall climbing season here on Mount Everest is almost over, and it looks like winter is well underway. In the ongoing battle of man versus mountain, score this round for mountain. Not a single climber has reached the summit, and the teams are heading home in defeat—all but a few diehards, who are hunkered down, sheltering from the storm. . . ."

As the man spoke, a huge burly form powered by, bent into the wind, carrying full gear—ice ax and heavy pack, spiked crampons on his feet. Despite the cumbersome load and terrible conditions, the climber moved with athletic ease. Just before he pulled his goggles over his eyes, his full face came into view.

Dan emitted a wheeze that matched the worst asthma attack of his life.

Hamilton Holt.

The Holts—the family of Cahills who had gotten

a jump on the next Clue—those Tomas muscleheads were climbing Mount Everest!

The frustration nearly dropped him where he stood in the video arcade. Now he knew where the next Clue was. And so what? He couldn't get in touch with Amy!

The sensation began at the base of his spine and expanded outward until it flooded his entire body. It was the feeling he'd had after Grace's funeral, when William McIntyre had told them all about the 39 Clues—urgent purpose, infinite possibility. A chance to become the most powerful person on earth, to shape human history! An opportunity so incredible that a pair of Boston orphans had turned down two million dollars for a place on the hunt.

Back then, it had been mostly Amy's call to chuck everything and join the contest. It was only a few weeks ago, but Dan had been through a lot since then. He'd traveled the world, experiencing thrills most people could only dream about. He'd nearly gotten killed at least a dozen times. That *changed* a guy. Life felt different after you'd looked death in the face.

He was not the same Dan Cahill—the one who'd wanted to take the money and buy baseball cards. He was now a full partner in the destiny Grace had set for them. How could he have been fool enough to let go of it? He could never quit the Clue hunt. He'd been *born* into it! Amy, too. And although there was no telling how many miles lay between them right now, as long as they were both on the trail of the 39 Clues, they were not truly separated.

The likes of Cora Wizard or Isabel Kabra could not be offered a chance at world domination.

I have to get to Mount Everest!

The arcade had a bank of computer workstations. Dan raced to an unoccupied one and opened the Internet browser. The manager rushed over and began yelling at him in Mandarin. Dan tossed a ball of crumpled Chinese bills onto the counter, hoping it would be enough to buy him some computer time.

Mount Everest . . . Mount Everest . . . there it was, on the border between Nepal and Tibet. And — okay, Tibet was in the southwest corner of China. Not close exactly, but at least he was in the same part of the world.

He Googled further. It was good to be back online. Amy felt comfortable surrounded by a stack of dusty books, but Dan was most at home surfing the web.

A railroad timetable came up on the screen. There it was — a train from Beijing, China, all the way to Lhasa, Tibet. One of the stops, about halfway along, was Xian. He grimaced at the schedule. Thirty hours?!

I'll go nuts!

Travel by air would be a lot faster, he reflected. But he had no passport and very little money.

And you can't stow away on a plane.

" . . . I'm in — well, I guess that doesn't matter, because I *have to find you guys now. Uh . . . see you later—I hope."*

Nellie stepped back from the pay phone at the Beijing airport, exhaling in sheer relief. The message was ten hours old, but Dan was alive! A little shaken up but okay. She couldn't wait to tell Amy.

The marathon that had brought them to this spot had been dizzying. A seven-mile sprint along the Great Wall to the bus staging area; an hour bus trip, which took three hours thanks to Beijing traffic; and a taxi ride out to the airport. All this carrying one very ticked-off cat.

Amy stepped out of the ladies' room and began to make her way through the crowded concourse. "Did you get the tickets?"

Nellie nodded grimly. "Brace yourself, kiddo. We can't get there till tomorrow."

"Huh? Why not?"

"You need a special travel permit for Tibet," the au pair explained. "They're letting us fly as far as Chengdu tonight. We can pick up the permits there tomorrow morning and grab the next plane to Lhasa. But there's bigger news. We got a message from Dan."

Amy's whoop echoed throughout the soaring curves of the terminal building. Heads turned their way. A security officer craned his neck to investigate the source of the disturbance.

Quickly, Nellie put an arm around Amy's shoulder and marched her to the pay phone so she could listen to the recording herself. She replayed the message four times before finally hanging up, trembling with emotion. "He sounds scared."

"Hey," Nellie's voice was kind but firm, "this is *good* news, remember? Of course he's scared. It looks like he's split with the Wizards. That's not so bad, either. Did you trust those sideshow freaks?"

"But he's all alone," Amy lamented. "Why didn't he tell us where to come and get him?"

"He had no way to be sure we'd get the message. For all he knew, he'd be waiting around for people who weren't going to show. We have to take him at his word that he's trying to find us." She shook her head helplessly. "God only knows how he's going to do that."

"By following the clue hunt," Amy said positively. The process of forcing herself to think logically was helping her control her emotions and focus her mind.

"Yeah, but you're talking about going to Mount Everest!"

Amy nodded grimly. "The mountain shape from the feng shui room—that's Everest—steep on one slope, more gradual on the other! Remember the list of headlines from the early twenties? George Mallory died high on Everest's north ridge in 1924! A lot of people believe he actually got to the top—that he was killed on the way down, not the way up."

"I've read about him," Nellie told her. "He was the guy who said he was climbing Everest 'because it is there.'"

Amy nodded. "I think he was climbing for another

reason, too. What if he was a Cahill, just like Puyi? In 1924, Puyi made some kind of breakthrough in the clue hunt. But he knew his days in the Forbidden City were numbered. So he arranged to have another Cahill hide the clue for him 'where the Earth meets the sky.' In other words, on top of the highest mountain in the world. Is that so impossible?"

"It's *totally* impossible!" Nellie raved. "It's the flimsiest, most insane fairy tale I've ever heard!" An odd expression came over her face. "In fact, it's just crazy enough to be the kind of thing that actually happens in your family. A regular hiding place isn't good enough for you Froot Loops; you have to use Mount Everest!"

"There could have been other factors," Amy suggested. "Everest is very cold; the air is thin; the atmospheric pressure is low. Puyi might have needed safe long-term storage."

"Well, here's something you might not have thought of," Nellie challenged. "Getting to Mount Everest is one thing. Getting to the top is another. You can't just walk up and start climbing. Even if the mountain doesn't stop you, the altitude will. People spend weeks acclimatizing. You go up too soon and it'll kill you!"

Amy smiled uncertainly. "I think I might have an idea about that."

In the search for the 39 Clues, Dan Cahill had been manhandled, half drowned, blown up, buried alive, and poisoned. But this was the most perilous of all.

He was being bored to death.

A thousand-mile journey on the slowest train in Asia, creeping across the continent one rattle at a time.

It had started out pretty well at the station in Xian. While the passengers were loading up the front coaches, Dan had managed to slip into a boxcar and hide behind sacks of rice. There he cowered, barely daring to breathe as a crew carried on more cargo.

Don't get caught. If they threw him off the train, there wasn't another one until tomorrow. He had no time to waste. This trip took long enough as it was.

Soon, though, the train was underway, and reality set in. Thirty hours stuck in this car, in the company of rice, a sleeping dog in a carrier, and—what was that over there? Oh, man, a coffin! His traveling companion was a dead guy.

With the passage of time, the casket became less creepy and more intriguing. By the fourth hour, Dan had convinced himself that he owed it to the dear departed to pay his respects by looking inside.

Empty. He was first relieved, then disappointed, then bored again. He checked his watch. Twenty-five and a half hours remained in the journey.

The worst part—even worse than the crushing boredom—was the fact that, while he was going out of his mind on the Turtle Express, the Holts were climbing Mount Everest in search of the Clue.

As the trip progressed, the train made a gradual

ascent onto the Tibetan plateau. Dan could not actually feel himself going up, but he did sense it in other ways — a splitting headache, fatigue, and a roaring thirst. The railway's website had warned about this. Lhasa, Tibet, the (end) of the line, was above eleven thousand feet. That took some getting used to for a Boston native who had lived most of his life at sea level.

He was also starving — to the point where he reached into the cage and stole a biscuit from the sleeping dog. It was disgusting — a meat-flavored cookie, with tons of salt, which parched him even further.

The slow ride became even slower, and the train squealed to a halt in yet another station. A second later, he heard voices and someone fumbling with the lock on the sliding door.

It left him with no time and no options. In a panic, he crawled into the coffin, pulling the lid shut after him. He was just in time. The boxcar door screeched wide, and footsteps and conversation filled the car. He lay there in abject misery, praying that he wouldn't have an asthma attack.

It was really no more than a few minutes, but it felt a lot longer. Finally, the heavy boxcar door slid shut and the train started off again. He pushed against the lid.

It didn't budge.

They locked me in here!

CHAPTER 21

Blind panic surged through him. He scrambled to his knees and began to push against the top with the strength of his entire body.

All at once, there was a clunk, and the resistance was gone. Dan exploded out of the casket as if he'd been fired from a missile silo. He landed in a heap on top of the rice bag that had been leaning on the coffin lid.

He tried to laugh it off. It wasn't funny.

He took stock of his surroundings. The dog was gone. No more meat cookies. In the pet carrier's place stood three tall stainless steel canisters. Something was sloshing inside of them. If it wasn't sulfuric acid, he was going to drink it.

He pried off the seal. Milk. Probably goat's, maybe even yak's. Definitely unpasteurized. Gross.

Nothing had ever tasted better.

At an altitude of 26,000 feet, the South Col of Everest was already higher than all but a handful of the world's mountains. This barren, rocky, storm-swept platform in the sky was formed in the place where Everest met its neighboring peak, Lhotse, creating the loftiest, coldest, least hospitable valley on the face of the earth.

It was a typical night on the Col — eighty below zero, with sustained winds that would have counted as a category two hurricane anyplace else.

"Isn't it beautiful, Ham?" shouted Eisenhower Holt over the howling of the gale. "A wind like this would toss an Ekat or a Lucian clean off the mountain! Finally the clue hunt comes around to something we Holts are good at!"

It was almost time for them to begin their push for the summit. On Everest, a team headed for the top in the middle of the night in order to arrive around midday with plenty of time to get back down again in daylight.

The Holts were looking forward to this with the joy of true athletes anticipating a monumental physical challenge. For most of the contest, they'd been out-maneuvered and outsmarted by their competition. Yet the Tomas had long known that George Mallory had been in cahoots with Emperor Puyi when the legendary mountaineer disappeared on Everest in 1924. What none of those smarty-pants branches had ever figured out was that Reginald Fleming Johnston, Puyi's tutor, had not been just a Janus scientist but also a cunning Tomas spy. Too cunning — Johnston had never revealed to anybody, not even his Tomas handlers, what Mallory had been carrying to the summit. It had taken some Holt-style persuasion, but Johnston's grandson had finally spilled the beans about what was up there. This prize would be more than enough to catapult the Holts into first place in the Clue hunt.

"I'm pumped!" Hamilton barked, and father and son bonked climbing helmets. "Reagan!" he bellowed at their tent. He switched on his flashlight and shone it in through the flap.

His sister Reagan, nearly as big and brawny as he was, crawled out onto the Col, zipping her wind suit. "Let's do this thing!" she cheered, and choked up momentarily. "I only wish poor Madison could be with us tonight."

"No, you don't!" Eisenhower boomed. "You're tickled pink that your sister got altitude sickness so you can hold it over her head forever!"

"She's not dead," Reagan defended herself. "A couple of days in a hyperbaric bag, and she'll be good as new."

"Save your breath," Eisenhower advised. "You're going to need it. They call it the Death Zone up here. Above twenty-five thousand feet, you're slowly dying — one cell at a time!"

It brought a cheer from his son and daughter. The Holts were all about living on the edge. And you couldn't get much more edgy than the Col, where, if you missed a step, the next one was more than a mile straight down.

"Oxygen!"

The three of them put masks over their noses and mouths and started toward Everest's looming summit pyramid, their crampons scraping on the barren rocks.

Greatness awaited above. The windchill was unimaginable; the altitude made every step a gasping, painful effort. But Eisenhower Holt might as well have been dancing through a garden of hyacinths. Gone was the humiliation of washing out at West Point. Gone was the myth that the Holts lacked the smarts to keep up with their illustrious family. Tonight, they were reaching for the sky. And nobody, Cahill or otherwise, stood between them and the top of the world.

They had not yet even reached the slope of the summit pyramid when another team passed them by, moving quickly across the Col. Four of the members were Sherpas — the stalwart Himalayan climbing guides who lived in the Khumbu Valley, the region around Everest on the Nepal side. They were accompanying a figure wearing what looked like a space suit.

Accompanying? They were practically carrying him! As the incline began, they were actually hoisting him under the arms as he moved forward. His high-tech costume pumped in oxygen and maintained the atmospheric pressure of sea level. Without it, anyone not acclimatized to Everest's thin air would have passed out in minutes.

The space-suited climber turned and waved at

the thunderstruck Holts. His face was clearly visible through the Plexiglas of his helmet.

Ian Kabra.

The Lhasa airport was only a fraction the size of Beijing's, and certainly not state of the art. It was even a lot smaller than Chengdu's, where Amy and Nellie had spent a miserable night trying to sleep on rows of benches, waiting for their travel papers for Tibet.

There was no jet bridge. The passengers exited the aircraft down portable stairs directly onto the tarmac. By the time they reached the terminal building, Nellie was out of breath, puffing from the effort of lugging her backpack and Saladin's pet carrier.

"Man, when this contest is over, I've got to get back to the gym. I'm way out of shape!"

"That's not it," Amy told her, a little breathless herself. "It's the altitude. Lhasa's over eleven thousand feet. And Tingri is even higher than that. It's not deadly like Everest, but we're going to feel the effects."

Nellie looked worried. "Couldn't we still get—you know—really sick?"

"Hopefully, we won't be here long enough for that to happen. The guidebook said it helps to drink a lot of water. Dehydration is a big part of it."

"I'll do my best," Nellie said sourly. "But good luck explaining all this to Saladin. He's such a crab anyway. This'll probably put him over the edge."

Their only stop was at a pay phone — no new message from Dan — before they trudged to the taxi line to ask about a very nonaverage ride.

Amy had been afraid it would be hard to find transportation to the village of Tingri, about three hours away. But the airport was crawling with taxis in search of business. When Nellie offered three hundred US dollars for the trip, it ignited a price war among the drivers, which brought the fare down to two hundred twenty-five.

Soon they were off with the lowest bidder, a perpetually smiling young man who spoke a little English. According to the ID certificate on the dashboard, his name was thirty-one letters long, but he introduced himself as Chip.

"Tingri. No problem. Near Chomolungma. You call Everest. Go climbing?"

"I hope not!" Nellie mumbled fervently. She turned to Amy. "You have a plan, right? We're not going all the way to Everest so we can stare at the top where the clue is, but not get there?"

"It's kind of a long shot," Amy admitted.

"That's not what I wanted to hear," the au pair put in.

"One of the reasons Everest is so dangerous is because most of the mountain is too high to be reached by rescue helicopter. The air is so thin that the rotor blades can't get any lift. But in 2005, the French developed an ultralight chopper, the A-Star, that landed for a few minutes on the summit. That helicopter is parked at an airfield outside Tingri."

Nellie regarded her with a mixture of admiration and wonder. "You're crazy — even for a Cahill! Who's going to fly the thing?"

"You have a pilot's license. I was thinking that, between the two of us, we could figure it out."

"I fly airplanes!" Nellie exploded. "Not some experimental Star Wars helicopter up Mount Everest!"

"I know it sounds nuts," Amy pleaded, "but I think this was meant to happen. Back in 2005, when the French landed that chopper on the summit, Grace made a huge deal out of it. She took Dan and me for the weekend, and we spent the whole time talking about the A-Star, reading about the A-Star, and watching the clips on YouTube. She *knew* we might have to do this one day. And when it came to the thirty-nine clues, Grace was never wrong."

"Except once," Nellie amended in a sober tone. "She thought she'd live longer so you poor kids wouldn't have to go through this alone."

CHAPTER 22

The yak cart creaked down the dirt lane on the outskirts of the village of Tingri in Xigaze Prefecture. It contained twigs for kindling, dried yak manure for heating fuel, and Dan Cahill.

He got out of the cart and handed over his last few coins to the driver. He was puffing on the thin air; his legs were so stiff they would barely support him; and he was flat broke in the middle of nowhere.

But he had made it! After a thirty-hour train ride, four hours on a smelly bus, and twenty minutes in the company of sticks and yak poop, he was actually at the helipad his grandmother had told him about.

The hangar was just an old barn. Only the French flag that doubled as a windsock hinted that this remote field was the home of the Ecureuil/A-Star 350, the helicopter that had landed on top of the world.

Everest. The peak towered over Dan as he approached the barn. Here it was only one feature in a titanic skyline, but it was the mightiest, the lord and master. The sight of it took his breath away—and breath was hard to come by at this altitude.

He peered in the window of the barn, knowing a brief moment of panic. What if it wasn't there? He'd come an awfully long way to find out that the helicopter was — God forbid — in the shop or something.

But no — there it was, looking just like the pictures Grace had shown him, futuristic and spare. The bubble was up, and someone was peering in at the instrument panel.

Why is it so dark in there? Why doesn't he just turn on a light?

Dan was about to knock on the door when he spotted the smashed padlock dangling from the hasp.

That guy's stealing my ultralight!

Without a moment's hesitation, Dan burst into the barn and brought down the intruder with a flying tackle. The two fell to the concrete floor in a struggling heap. A flailing elbow hit Dan in the mouth, and he tasted blood. Enraged, he reached around and pressed the heel of his hand into his opponent's face. He was encouraged to note that the intruder was not much bigger than he was, and about equal in strength.

Suddenly, pain shot through his hand, and he howled in shock.

He bit me!

They wrestled, rolling one over the other, until Dan found his face pressed against a metal grill, eyes staring in at —

"Saladin?"

His opponent's grip disintegrated. *"Dan?"*

"Amy?"

"Oh, God!" Nellie dropped the crowbar she was just about to bring down on Dan's head.

The two Cahills scrambled up, each one goggling as if the sight of the other was a mirage. Then they were together in an ecstatic bear hug.

"Cut it out!" Dan complained. "You're strangling me!" But he didn't loosen his grip on his sister.

Amy had been so worried for so long that the sudden evaporation of tension left her boneless. If she let go, she probably would have collapsed in a heap. "I thought I'd lost you! Just like we lost Mom and Dad!"

"Why didn't you look for me?" Dan babbled.

"We did! We never stopped!"

"Oh, yeah? Then what are you doing here?"

"Well, it must have been exactly the right place!" Amy snapped. "You showed up, didn't you?"

"I caught the Holts on TV!" Dan pulled away. "Stop yelling at me! I missed you *so* much! I thought I'd never see you again!" He scanned the hangar. "And if you lost my computer—"

Amy struggled to regain her composure. "You look taller," she said finally, devouring him with her eyes.

"Don't be an idiot. It was only five days."

"I know . . ." There was a tremor in her voice. "But it was a very *long* five days. Dan, I'm so sorry—" And then his words percolated down to her. "Wait a minute! The Holts were on TV?"

"They're climbing Mount Everest!" Dan exclaimed. "Like, *right now*! There has to be a clue up there!"

Amy turned back to the A-Star. "We can beat them to the top. Right, Nellie?"

"Wrong," the au pair said sadly. "I'm sorry, you guys, but there's no way I can fly this thing. It looks more like a cat's cradle than an aircraft. I'd get us all killed for sure."

Amy and Dan regarded each other with anguish. Had fate brought them to the same spot in this tiny village in Everest's shadow only to stymie them now?

At that moment, the lights flashed on and a sharp voice rang out: "*Que faites-vous ici?* What are you doing here?"

Startled, the three turned to face the newcomer, a short, gaunt, middle-aged man in pilot's coveralls.

Shy Amy was tongue-tied. Not so Dan. "We need to go up Mount Everest," he blurted.

The man laughed out loud. "I do not run a tourist service. If it is pretty pictures you want, they sell postcards in the village."

Amy found her voice. "No, he means we have to go to the summit. Right away."

The man's eyes narrowed. "Ah, so you know what the A-Star is capable of. *Alors*, this is impossible. Leave the property at once."

"We'll pay," said Nellie.

The man scowled. "The A-Star is a piece of technology unique in all the world. You do not rent it like a Jet Ski for one hour at the beach."

The Cahills' despair was palpable. Up until now, they'd succeeded by thinking on their feet, improvising, and overcoming obstacles. This was different. There was only one quick way up Mount Everest — one that avoided the months of training, provisioning, acclimatizing, and climbing. It was this helicopter, period. The laws of science and nature provided no plan B. If the pilot refused to take them, what then?

Nellie indicated the satellite phone on the corner of the workbench. "Let me call my boss. Maybe we can work something out."

Amy and Dan exchanged bewildered glances. As far as they knew, Nellie's boss was their Aunt Beatrice, Grace's sister, technically their guardian. Aunt Beatrice was so cheap that she wouldn't spring for cable TV, much less a helicopter to the earth's pinnacle.

The pilot was disgusted. "You Americans think everything can be bought with your *money*!"

"One call," Nellie persisted.

There was a confidence and authority in her voice that Amy and Dan hadn't heard before. Their au pair had always been helpful — occasionally a lifesaver. But she'd always taken a backseat in the Clue hunt. Something was different now.

"Listen to what my boss has to say," Nellie went

on. "I really think it'll be worth your while."

He looked aggrieved but gestured toward the sat phone.

She punched in the numbers and waited for the satellite connection to be made.

"Sorry to wake you up, sir. Yes, I do know what time it is there." Quickly, she outlined their situation and then passed the handset to the Frenchman. "He wants to talk to you."

Amy and Dan watched intently as the pilot listened to the voice many thousands of miles away. His eyes widened; his expression grew increasingly awed. He did not say a single word; just handed the phone back to Nellie and announced, "We depart in ten minutes!"

As the man set about the preflight preparations, Amy sidled up to the au pair. "Who did you call?"

Nellie shrugged. "My uncle. He's a pretty persuasive person."

"But what did he say? Did he bribe the guy?"

"How should I know?" the au pair retorted. "I wasn't part of the conversation." She glared at them, as if daring them to question her further.

The Cahills knew better than to second-guess the person who finagled them a ride up Everest. Yet Amy couldn't hold back. "Are you ever going to tell us who you really are?"

Nellie hesitated. "I'm your babysitter —"

"Au pair," Dan corrected automatically.

She gathered them into her arms. *"And* your friend," she finished. But the expression on her face was strangely guilty. "You'd better get ready. This is your one shot."

The pilot helped brother and sister into GORE-TEX wind suits and provided them with boots and gloves. The temperature at the Everest summit could reach triple digits below zero, even without factoring in the wind, which averaged 120 miles per hour.

Breathing apparatus was next — face masks connected to cylinders that were harnessed to their backs. The rigs were awkward and uncomfortable. Dan couldn't escape the feeling of a mild yet never-ending asthma attack, and Amy was unnerved by the sound of her own breath reverberating in her ears. But the equipment was absolutely necessary. At 29,035 feet, the air contained only one-third as much oxygen as at sea level. Without supplemental Os, they would not last thirty seconds.

Finally, the pilot carefully weighed them on a scale. In the impossibly thin air and low pressure, every ounce was critical. A few extra pounds could make the difference between a clean takeoff and being stranded in a place where no one could survive for long.

Nellie stepped forward. "My turn."

"This is the famous American sense of humor, no?" the Frenchman exclaimed in disbelief. "We cannot accommodate another milligram. It is only because these two are children that I can take them both without risking all our lives."

"It's my job to look out for their safety!" the au pair protested.

"In that case, your incompetence is beyond measure," the pilot told her without hesitation. "Where we journey, safety is a word truly without meaning. Now, do we go, or do we not?"

"We go," Amy said, hoping she sounded decisive rather than just plain scared. "Otherwise we're handing this clue to the Holts."

They opened the hangar doors, and the A-Star was wheeled out onto the helipad on a rolling skid. It was so light that the pilot was able to move it on his own, mostly because he did not trust anyone else to touch it. The low-density metals and polymers were so delicate that "clumsy children might compromise the integrity of the craft."

Their seats took up less space than the seat belts that buckled them in. The helicopter was as minimal and empty as it could possibly be.

Nellie turned to her charges. "Promise me you won't do anything crazy."

The Cahills were too cowed to respond. Besides, it was already past time for promises. It didn't get much crazier than what they were about to do.

Nellie backed away, and the rotor blade began to turn, slowly at first, then picking up speed. The A-Star lifted off the Tibetan plateau.

Next stop: the planet's zenith — a jagged spike of ice and rock nearly three miles above them.

CHAPTER 23

The Hillary Step was a fifty-five-foot cliff in the sky—Mount Everest's last cruel joke on its exhausted, breathless, hypothermic climbers. At a lower altitude, it would have presented a minor obstacle to a seasoned mountaineer. But at nearly 29,000 feet—well above the summit of K-2, the world's second-highest peak—each tiny movement was a guided tour through a world of pain.

The three bone-weary Holts watched in dismay as Ian Kabra's Sherpa team dragged their Lucian rival up the Step, literally carrying him as they ascended the tangle of fixed ropes left over from decades of expeditions.

"No fair!" bawled Hamilton. What would normally have been a bellow barely made it past the plastic of his oxygen mask.

"Lucian cheater!" panted Reagan.

Their Tomas strength had enabled the Holts to acclimatize for the Himalayan ascent in a fraction of the usual time. Yet they were still subject to Everest's merciless ravages. The three were exhausted, freezing, dehydrated, and oxygen starved. Ian, by contrast, was warm and comfortable in his space suit. And thanks to his Sherpa bearers, he probably wasn't even very tired.

The summit ridge was blanketed in waist-deep snow from the recent blizzards. The Holts were swimming the mountain as much as climbing it. Reagan was now thinking enviously of her sister's hospital bed. She knew she couldn't go much farther.

Eisenhower Holt let out a howl of pure emotion that started a small avalanche on the Step. They were *not* going to lose to those Kabras again! When he spoke, the focus of a champion athlete was unmistakable behind his crushing fatigue.

"Kids, we don't get much respect from the rest of the family. But we're part of a great tradition, stretching back five hundred years to Thomas Cahill himself. Ham, stay with your sister. I'm going to show the world what the Tomas can do!"

He took off through the deep snowdrifts, a study in determination and raw power. He hit the ropes of the Hillary Step, climbing hand over hand without pausing for rest. Any mountaineer would have claimed it was physically impossible.

There were no such words in the Holt vocabulary.

At the top, he disappeared into the blowing snow, but they heard his booming voice: *"Eat my dust, Kabra!"*

"He's ahead!" Reagan croaked.

Hamilton nodded in admiration and pride. He'd spent most of his life thinking of his father as kind of a boob. But here on Mount Everest, Eisenhower Holt was the boob you wanted on your side.

"No one can beat him to the summit now!"

The Ecureuil/A-Star 350 climbed higher and higher into the thin air, soaring past altitudes far beyond the ceiling of any other helicopter in the world.

For Amy and Dan, who had been through some pretty terrifying experiences, this was the ultimate terror. The A-Star was so tiny and insubstantial that they felt completely unprotected, as if this were some demented theme park ride, out in the open, six miles above sea level.

The brutal Himalayan winds buffeted the ultralight craft, tossing it around like a Ping-Pong ball in a hurricane. Amy and Dan clutched at each other because there was literally nothing else to hold on to.

The closer they got to the mountain, the more defined Everest became from its neighbors — higher, massive, with a distinctive white plume streaming from its peak.

"Is that a cloud?" Dan asked, shouting to get the words past his breathing apparatus.

Their pilot provided the answer. "The top of Everest reaches into the jet stream," he called back. "What you see are millions of ice crystals blowing off the summit.

I told you this was no sightseeing tour. Prepare for what you Americans call a bumpy ride."

It was no exaggeration. The closer they got to the summit, the more ferocious the gyrations of the A-Star became.

"How are we going to land?" Amy shrilled in a panic. "We'll crash into the mountain!"

The pilot's upper body shook, as if the controls were manipulating him rather than the other way around. Except for the turbulence, they were barely moving now, trying to hover over the peak. Suddenly, the world disappeared as they passed through the ice plume. They were flying blind at the very edge of the atmosphere.

A sudden drop and bump drew screams from both Cahills.

"What happened?" Dan wailed.

"You wanted the summit; you are there," the pilot informed them. He indicated the altimeter: 29,035 feet. There could be no higher reading. Not on earth.

"We — we made it?" Amy stammered. She had fully expected to be smashed to pieces far below.

"*Vite!* Hurry!" he ordered. "We have five minutes at the most! I cannot shut down the engine for fear it will not restart!" With a pop, he opened the bubble.

Amy and Dan wasted precious seconds unclipping their belts and struggling out of the A-Star. They'd had a zero percent expectation of making it this far, so there was no concrete plan of what to do now.

The search for the 39 Clues had brought them to some

amazing places, but the summit of Mount Everest literally topped them all. The cold was indescribable, the wind an unrelenting onslaught. They had to crawl away from the chopper to get clear of the rotor blades. Even with supplemental oxygen from their masks, the effort left them gasping for air that simply wasn't there.

Yet nothing could move Amy's mind from the magnificence of this spot. "Everything's *down*!" she exclaimed in wonder. "There's no up anymore! Even the clouds are below us!"

The world's pinnacle! No amount of research could have prepared her for this spectacular place. Gargantuan peaks rose all around, but their perch was the highest of all, dominating the planet's loftiest neighborhood. Lhotse, at nearly twenty-eight thousand feet, seemed far beneath them. The sky was an incredible, unnaturally deep cobalt blue. At this altitude, they were at the edge of the earth's troposphere, not far from the beginning of outer space.

As Dan's boots crunched the snow on the roof of the world, he tossed over his shoulder at the pilot, "If you leave us here, that dude on the phone is going to be really ticked off!" He had no idea who "that dude" might be — obviously not Nellie's uncle. But there could be no question about the person's power and influence.

"Can you believe where we are?" Amy shouted over the roar of the jet stream.

"Awesome!" Dan tore his eyes from the view and concentrated on the terrain of the summit. The sight jarred him. "Hey, this is a garbage dump!"

A spaghetti of colorful Buddhist prayer flags flapped fiercely in the gale. There were also dozens of national flags. Empty oxygen cylinders were scattered everywhere. And buried in the snow was an oddball collection of objects and knickknacks, everything from framed family photographs to pieces of jewelry and even toys.

Dan was bewildered. "Who brought all this stuff up here?"

"They're souvenirs," Amy explained breathlessly. "Every climber wants to leave something on the summit. The question is, what did Mallory leave?"

Dan picked up a locket and opened it to reveal a faded snapshot of a fat baby. "How do we know which of this junk is the clue? We've only got five minutes, Amy! We're probably down to four now!"

Amy thought hard. "Mallory was here first, so whatever he brought must be on the bottom. We dig."

They began to scrabble at the snow, clearing away dense powder littered with hundreds of random items. Farther down, the snow was packed a little harder, and Amy grabbed a large picture frame to function as a shovel while Dan pounded with a spent oxygen bottle, using it as a hammer. Luckily, there were no major ice formations, thanks to the jet stream, which ripped off most of the moisture.

At this altitude, an ironman triathlon was packed into every simple movement. Within seconds, both were wheezing and coughing violently. Human bodies were not meant to survive in these conditions, much less work hard. Amy could sense her vision constricting as her brain screamed for more oxygen. She bit down painfully on the side of her mouth to stay alert and focused. On Everest, mental exhaustion could be just as deadly as the physical kind.

"If we dig much more," Dan puffed, "K-2 may have to take over as the world's tallest mountain!"

"I don't think we need to worry about that," Amy gasped. "Look—already there's a lot less stuff buried here. We're getting down to the layers from the very earliest Everest expeditions."

"Two minutes!" came a shout from the ultralight.

Against all odds, they sped up. Dan pounded wildly with the cylinder, and Amy sifted with icy fingers, discarding amulets and St. Christopher medals. It had been difficult enough getting here. To run out of time before they could find the Clue was unthinkable.

"Stop!" she screamed suddenly.

Dan froze in midair, the cylinder poised inches from a small half-buried glass vial.

Delicately, Amy cleared away the surrounding snow and drew out the bottle. It was a thick glass container, tightly corked, its contents frozen.

On one flat surface was a Chinese chop that Amy recognized instantly. She unzipped her wind suit, reached inside her shirt, and pulled out the folded silk from the Forbidden City. The wind nearly ripped it from her hand, but she kept a death grip on it. Together, she and Dan managed to get it opened up.

"That's the chop of Puyi, the last emperor!" she shouted into the gale. "It's a perfect match, see? Puyi gave this to George Mallory to hide for him!"

"But what's in the bottle?" Dan asked.

"Remember the vial from Paris—the one the Kabras stole? I think this might be something similar." She turned over the bottle. Etched into the other side was the symbol of the standing wolf—the Janus crest.

The rush of discovery had blood pounding in her ears loud enough to drown out the howling jet stream. "Dan, I've got it!" She pointed to the pictures on the silk—the "equation" made from the family symbols. "This doesn't mean that the family is the sum of its branches. Look at the shapes around those crests! They're vials, just like this one and the one from Paris! There are four chemical formulas—one for each branch. And when you mix them all together, they make some kind of master serum! That's what the thirty-nine clues are—the ingredients to that serum!"

"One minute!" bellowed the pilot.

Not even the fact that they were running out of time could distract them as the truth about the 39 Clues began to reveal itself.

"Think about the family branches and what they're good at!" Amy went on. "The Lucians are masters of strategy and cunning; the Janus are creative and dramatic; the Tomas are athletic and strong; and the

Ekats can invent anything. And those traits have been passed on from generation to generation, so the chemical effect must actually become part of your DNA. With the master serum, you'd be all those things at the same time! You'd be unbeatable!"

There was a silent exchange between the two of them. A formula that powerful in the wrong hands . . .

"Thirty seconds!" The pilot was practically hysterical. "If you are coming, the time is *now*!"

Dan helped Amy wrestle the blowing silk back into her wind suit and ran. Amy was about to follow him when the snow-reflected sun glinted off one more inscription on the bottle, this one much smaller than the others. She held it up to her goggles and squinted at the bottom of the vial.

The message had been scratched into the glass, probably by pen knife, or perhaps the edge of an ice ax. It read:

GM — George Mallory. Generations of adventurers had been inspired by his legendary words — that he was climbing Everest "because it is here." But he hadn't been talking about the peak at all! He'd meant the Janus serum—and the one place on earth where it would be safe.

Her energy was nearly gone, sapped by the altitude and the herculean feat of digging at twenty-nine thousand feet. Hands trembling, she clutched the vial, final proof of the collaboration between two Cahills separated by thousands of miles. The conspirators could not possibly have been more different. One an emperor, the last of a glorious dynasty that dated back centuries; the other a simple British schoolteacher who climbed mountains as a hobby. What had it taken to bring them together? Nothing less than the 39 Clues.

"Ten seconds!!"

"Come on, Amy!" Dan grabbed her arm, jolting her out of her reverie. The two dropped to the snow, scrambled under the ultralight's whirling rotor, and dived through the opening in the bubble.

"Go! Go! Go!" Dan croaked.

The pilot worked the controls. There was a grinding sound, and the A-Star resisted for an instant, its rotor struggling to coax some lift from the nonexistent air. At last, the ultralight slowly began to rise from the world's highest peak.

"I can't believe we did it!" breathed Amy.

And then a very large gloved hand closed on the A-Star's left runner.

CHAPTER 24

Their ascent halted. The chopper began to shake violently.

"What is this malfunction?" the pilot yelled.

Roaring with effort, Eisenhower Holt pulled down on the runner, preventing their departure.

"It's not a malfunction, it's a Holt!" Dan cried. "Keep flying! He'll have to let go!"

"He is too heavy for this altitude!" the pilot insisted. "He wastes our fuel! We must depart now if we are to get home at all!"

Still holding on with one hand, Eisenhower swung his ice ax and wedged the sharp point in the gasket between the ultralight and its bubble. Then he pried with all his remaining strength until the Plexiglas popped open. A split second later, his enormous frost-bitten, wild-eyed head loomed directly over them.

"The clue!" he roared. As Amy sat petrified with fear, her Holt cousin snatched the vial from her nerveless fingers. He backed off, releasing the chopper.

He got three steps from that spot. Four Sherpas

appeared out of the ice plume and grabbed him, two on each arm. A fifth figure, the space-suited Ian Kabra, staggered up against the wind and wrenched the vial from Eisenhower's glove.

What happened next would remain burned in everyone's memory. A blast of wind seized the A-Star and pitched it around. Dan tumbled from his seat, whacking his head on the Plexiglas bubble. Amy was tossed clean out, landing in the snow. The tail of the chopper swung over earth's pinnacle, whacking Ian across his back, knocking him off the summit.

He flailed for a handhold, digging the arms of his space suit into a snow cornice. Screaming in horror, he clung to the edge, dangling over the massive Kangshung face, a drop of eleven thousand feet.

Amy grabbed for his hand and found herself holding not Ian, but the vial containing the Janus serum.

Her first thought was jubilation. *I've got it back!*

But then she looked through the space suit helmet at the terrified face of the teenager inside.

Suddenly, the ledge of packed powder that was supporting Ian crumbled under his weight.

There was nothing beneath him for nearly two miles.

Amy's decision was instant. She dropped the Janus serum and clamped both hands on Ian's arm. The vial plunged down the face, disappearing from sight long before it shattered far below. The Sherpas joined her, and Ian was hauled back to the safety of the summit.

Amy had no more breath. Even as she sprinted for the ultralight, she knew it was too late. She was running on empty, already collapsing, the snow of the summit swinging up to meet her. . . .

Dan clamped his arms around his sister and hauled her bodily into the A-Star. As they tumbled aboard, the pilot reached up and closed the bubble. With a lurch, the little craft left Everest behind.

"The serum!" Dan asked anxiously.

Amy shook her head, awareness returning. "Smashed." She regarded her brother apologetically. "I couldn't let him die."

As soon as the words were out of her mouth, she realized the importance of what she'd just said. "Dan — I had a choice! And I saved Isabel Kabra's son!"

"Don't remind me," Dan said through clenched teeth. "The next time Ian and Natalie feed me to a lollipop machine, I'll know who to thank."

"Don't you get it?" Amy persisted. "If the Madrigals were as bad as everybody says, I would have saved the bottle, not Ian! I did the human thing." She looked at him earnestly. "We don't have to be evil just because we're Madrigals. Madrigals are horrible—but we can change our destiny."

"What about Mom and Dad?" asked Dan.

"I don't know. . . ." If Amy had learned one lesson from the Clue hunt and its many deceptions, it was to value truth above all. She would have given anything to believe that their parents were good people. But her eyes met Dan's, and the name beamed between them as if by radar: *Nudelman.*

"I wouldn't have let Ian die, either," Dan admitted after a solemn pause. "I just hate losing the serum. Especially since we didn't even get a clue out of this."

Amy smiled broadly. "Yes, we did. We've had it since the Forbidden City," She told him. "I just didn't understand it until now. Alistair translated Puyi's poem:

'That which you seek, you hold in your hand,
Fixed forever in birth,
Where the Earth meets the sky.'"

"I understand the 'Earth meets sky' part," said Dan. "But holding it in your hand? The only thing you could be holding is the sheet with the poem on it."

"Which is silk," Amy added, eyes alight. "Silk is spun by the silkworm, which is really—"

"The *Bombyx mori* caterpillar," her brother supplied, thinking of snack time at the Shaolin Temple. "It tastes like chicken."

She gave him a strange look and went on. "The stuff comes out liquid and solidifies into silk filament when it hits the air. But the ingredient is 'fixed forever in birth.' In other words, the silk in its liquid form—raw silkworm secretion."

Dan shook his head in wonder. "And Puyi didn't have a freezer, so he got Mallory to stick it up on Mount Everest for him. Wow!"

Amy nodded. "Can you imagine what must have been going through Mallory's head when he planted that vial on the summit eighty-six years ago? He'd just conquered Everest—and he did it twenty-nine years before Sir Edmund Hillary in 1953." She paused ruefully. "Little did the poor guy realize that he was going to die on the way down. He's still on the mountain, you know. His body is frozen solid, so he's always going to be there."

"Cool," said Dan. "I mean, not the being dead part. But, you know—the spot of his greatest triumph becomes his final resting place. It makes sense."

Amy regarded him with disapproval. "I'd forgotten how weird you are."

The pilot's voice intruded on their conversation.

"Since neither of you American hotshots bothered to ask if we have enough fuel to land, the answer is yes. Barely."

"That's great news!" Amy exclaimed, embarrassed. "Thank you for the—uh—ride."

"*De rien, mademoiselle.* You have powerful friends. At least, your companion with the nose ring does."

"Yeah, what's up with that?" Dan mused. "How many au pairs could make a phone call and score you a ticket up Everest in an experimental chopper?"

"She's definitely more than a regular au pair," Amy agreed. "You should have seen her at the Great Wall. She picked a lock like a pro." Her expression softened. "But whatever else she is, she's on our side. I think."

They looked back at Everest, silent and severe in its powerful majesty.

"Did you ever dream of being up there?" Amy asked in a hushed tone.

"Sure," Dan enthused. "All the time. One day I'm going to climb it."

She made a face. "Be sure to send me a postcard."

They were low enough to make out the village of Tingri now, a small collection of ancient buildings on the vast Tibetan plateau. A mile or so outside of town, the helipad came into view, and, standing outside, Nellie was shading her eyes as she scanned the sky. Not far from her, a tiny gray dot—Saladin.

Family, waiting to welcome them home. For two orphans, that was something you couldn't put a price on.

CHAPTER 26

In the underground parking garage of the Bell Tower Hotel in Xian, China, Jonah Wizard emerged from his limo just in time to see a six-foot terracotta warrior figure being loaded carefully onto a truck by two uniformed workmen.

"Hey, where'd you get—?"

The words were barely out of his mouth when a second warrior was toted by, this time under the supervision of Cora Wizard.

"Mom—where did these come from?"

"We're the Janus," she explained. "Do you really think we can't whip up a few statues to replace the ones you broke? *Careful with that!*" she snapped as one of the porters sideswiped a pillar. "It's supposed to look two thousand years old, not two million!"

She turned back to her son. "I've been thinking about your request to be relieved of your responsibilities in the clue hunt."

"And?" he prompted anxiously.

In answer, her hand came around and slapped him

across the face hard enough to send him sprawling.

He scrambled up again. "What's up with that, yo?"

"I am not 'yo,'" Cora Wizard said through clenched teeth. "I am the head of this branch, which is bigger than you or I or Mozart or Jane Cahill herself. The future of our kind, from Spielberg to the lowliest juggler on a unicycle, lies in the thirty-nine clues, and I won't allow my son or anyone else to take the Janus out of the running for this prize. Especially now that we know there are Madrigals involved."

"Are you sure about that?" Jonah challenged. "What if the kid was just blowing smoke?"

"I should have figured it out years ago," she berated herself. "No wonder Grace and her oh-so-perfect daughter never allied themselves with one of the branches. We all thought it was part of their high-and-mighty routine — always above the fray, never dirtying their hands. And all this time, they were the lowest of the low."

"I'm not cut out for the clue hunt, Mom," Jonah pleaded. "I'm not good at it."

"You are Janus," his mother said firmly. "You are more gifted and brilliant than all the Lucian, Tomas, and Ekat troglodytes put together. For centuries, we have played second fiddle to those Lucian butchers, when our qualities dwarf theirs. And do you want to know the reason?"

He stared at her, totally abashed.

"The reason is that Lucians stop at nothing to achieve their goals. They lie, they cheat, they steal." Her laser-guided eyes locked with her son's. "And they kill."

Jonah Wizard had spent his entire life in service to the Janus branch. On their instructions, he had become a rapper, a TV star, and an international mogul.

He had no doubt what was expected of him next.

With the fall climbing season over, Tingri wasn't much of a tourist attraction, so they had the guesthouse all to themselves. Amy, Dan, and Nellie sat around the open fire pit in the kitchen, completely exhausted, but too excited to sleep. Saladin had no such problem. He was curled up on the hearth and hadn't moved for hours.

"This is *wonderful*," Nellie murmured contentedly. "The heat of the fire, the cold, dry air. Someone ought to open a resort in Tingri. Even the smoke smells richer, earthier. Maybe it's the altitude."

Dan laughed without humor. "Maybe it's the yak poop. That's what they heat with up here."

"And cook, too?" Amy asked in dismay. She pushed away her cup of sweet aromatic tea.

They had spent the evening filling each other in on their separate adventures throughout China, marveling at how such different paths had brought the two of them to the foot of Everest at almost the same moment.

Dan howled with delight at Amy's description of Saladin's plunge off the Great Wall. And Amy laughed just as hard when Dan tried to convince her that their cousin Jonah wasn't all bad.

"Seriously," he insisted, "you've got to feel sorry for someone who's trying to live up to guys like Mozart and Rembrandt. And that mother! He could sell a trillion CDs, and it would never be good enough for her. She's like a cross between Aunt Beatrice and Medusa. Man, she practically swallowed her own head when I told her we were Madrigals."

Amy drew in a sharp breath. "You told her that?"

"I couldn't help it. I was just too mad."

She nodded. "I hear you. But you know how the Cahills feel about Madrigals. The other teams will be gunning for us twice as much as before. We have no idea where to look for the next clue. And which of our darling cousins will be willing to trade information with us now? Nobody would form an alliance with a Madrigal."

Dan looked crestfallen, then suddenly leaped to his feet. "Wait a minute! Maybe we're not so dead in the water. Remember the Beard Buddha from Grace's house? Well, the real thing is on Mount Song. In a cave behind it, I found these ancient burned-up pieces of lab equipment. Wasn't Gideon Cahill's lab destroyed in a fire?"

Amy nodded, intrigued. "Where's all that stuff now?"

"It was too much to bring, so I re-hid it. But there

was one thing I couldn't leave." He reached into the pocket of his jeans and drew out the painted miniature in the gold frame.

Amy was thunderstruck. "A picture of *Mom*?"

"Look closer. The clothes, the hair. That's not Mom. It's old. Maybe centuries old."

Amy took the miniature and peered at it. "An ancestor, then."

"A *Cahill* ancestor," Dan amended. "And when you've got Cahills—"

"They're usually mixed up in the thirty-nine clues." Amy gently pried the oval miniature out of the frame. The portrait was unmarked and unsigned. But engraved on the inside of the frame was: PROPERTY OF ANNE BONNY.

"Anne Bonny!" Amy repeated. "She was a pirate in the Caribbean—the most notorious female pirate ever! Was she a Cahill?"

"Only one way to find out," replied Dan. "Looks like we're going to the Caribbean."

Nellie, who had been dozing, sat bolt upright in her chair. "Did somebody say Caribbean?"

"The next clue might be there," Amy confirmed.

"Now, that's more like it!" Nellie crowed. "Number thirty-five sunblock, bikinis, beach time, drinks served in coconuts—I'm so in!"

Outside the guesthouse, the shadowy hulk of Everest loomed over them, now holding one less secret.

YOU COULD INSTANTLY WIN** AN INTERNATIONAL GETAWAY!

MOSCOW

PARIS

VENICE

BOSTON

TOKYO

BAHAMAS

Race to Win!

Log on to www.the39clues.com and add any new The 39 Clues book or game card to your online account between April 6 and August 30, 2010 and you could be eligible to
INSTANTLY WIN a family trip to a worldwide The 39 Clues location.

5 grand-prize winners will each receive:

- **4 round-trip airline tickets** to one of a selection of The 39 Clues destinations*: Bahamas, Boston, Moscow, Paris, Tokyo, or Venice

- **A $5,000 American Express Gift Card** to cover all other trip expenses

The hunt is on and there's a race to win...are you in?

For More Details Visit
www.the39clues.com/racetowin

■ SCHOLASTIC

39CWINL

William,

All falls into place. Cahills across the globe embrace
their destiny and begin the hunt for the 39 Clues.
More join the hunt with each hour, but for the plan
to work, still more are needed.

Continue your work, William. Convince the young
Cahills that they just might conquer the world.

Imagine if they knew the truth.

—F

How to Start

1. Go to www.the39clues.com

2. Click on "Join Now" and choose a username and password.

3. Explore the Cahill world and track down Clues.

There are over $100,000 in prizes for lucky Clue hunters.

Read the Books. Collect the Cards. Play the Game. Win the Prizes